"Let me do my job. Your whole team is working on this."

A sad smile pulled at her mouth. "Of course they are."

"All you need to do is stay as safe as possible until I can get everyone released. I'll do whatever is necessary to get you out of there."

"I know you will. You're the best."

This was the one time he would give anything to rise to the expectations of his reputation. It was a lot to live up to. A lot for someone to be. More so when it came to people in his life.

He had believed they could have carried on casually, indefinitely, with neither risking the pain of getting their hearts involved.

What a fool he'd been.

WYOMING MOUNTAIN HOSTAGE

Juno Rushdan

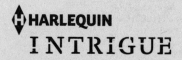

This is for the ones I love. You know who you are.

HARLEQUIN®
INTRIGUE™

ISBN-13: 978-1-335-58261-4

Wyoming Mountain Hostage

Copyright © 2023 by Juno Rushdan

For questions and comments about the quality of this book, please contact us at CustomerService@Harlequin.com.

Harlequin Enterprises ULC
22 Adelaide St. West, 41st Floor
Toronto, Ontario M5H 4E3, Canada
www.Harlequin.com

Printed in U.S.A.

Juno Rushdan is a veteran US Air Force intelligence officer and award-winning author. Her books are action-packed and fast-paced. Critics from *Kirkus* and *Library Journal* have called her work "heart-pounding James Bond-ian adventure" that "will captivate lovers of romantic thrillers." For a free book, visit her website: www.junorushdan.com.

Books by Juno Rushdan

Harlequin Intrigue

Cowboy State Lawmen

Wyoming Winter Rescue
Wyoming Christmas Stalker
Wyoming Mountain Hostage

Fugitive Heroes: Topaz Unit

Rogue Christmas Operation
Alaskan Christmas Escape
Disavowed in Wyoming
An Operative's Last Stand

A Hard Core Justice Thriller

Hostile Pursuit
Witness Security Breach
High-Priority Asset
Innocent Hostage
Unsuspecting Target

Tracing a Kidnapper

Visit the Author Profile page at Harlequin.com.

CAST OF CHARACTERS

FBI special agent Jake Delgado—This cowboy law enforcement officer is thrust into danger right after finding out that he is about to become a father and the mother of his child is taken hostage.

Special agent Rebecca "Becca" Hammond—When she is taken hostage, she is drawn into a conspiracy that threatens her, the life of her child and everyone in town.

Crispin Lund—A pillar of the community who may have something to hide.

Nash Garner—The best friend and coworker of Jake Delgado. He recently asked his friend's sister to marry him.

Lynn Delgado—She will do anything to help her brother, including asking her fiancé to bend the rules.

Cameron Lund—A high school librarian. Is he innocent or does he know more than he is saying?

Chapter One

This was the last thing Jake Delgado had expected. Or wanted.

On the two-and-a-half-hour drive from Denver to Laramie, Wyoming, he had been fantasizing about having a good time with Becca Hammond, a fellow FBI agent and his occasional hookup. Friends-with-benefits was not applicable since they had never quite been friends. So, having the "where do we stand" talk had *not* been on his agenda tonight.

"Are you listening to me?" Becca asked.

"Yeah, of course, I am. I was just looking at that vehicle again." Jake gestured through the windshield at the nondescript white van that circled the Laramie Public Library, where they were parked near the rear entrance. "That's their second time around."

The van had entered off the side street of Seventh, cutting through the L-shaped parking lot, and was heading toward Grand Avenue, where the other entrance was located.

"Probably someone waiting to pick someone up, the same as us," she said, frustration sharpening her voice.

"I'm trying to talk to you. This is important. Can you at least look at me?"

Becca was wound tighter than he had ever seen her. She hadn't even glanced at the van. This was a quiet, small community surrounded by breathtaking mountains. An idyllic haven where the violent crime rate was low enough to get a good agent to drop their guard. It was the kind of place where neighbors got to know each other, where help if you needed it during difficult situations could easily be found. Still, he mentally noted the license plate number before giving her his full attention, which only made his predicament worse.

She was stunning. Utterly breathtaking. Curly auburn hair that was as fiery as her spirit. Creamy skin. A heart-shaped face. Pronounced cheekbones. Deep brown eyes burning hot with annoyance rather than the passion he had been hoping for when he'd arranged to take this half day as well as tomorrow off for a long weekend with her. The least she could've done was given him a heads-up about this instead of blindsiding him.

His gaze dipped to her sexy attire. She had changed from the usual stiff suit she wore to work into a short, flowy dress with vibrant flowers that he wanted to pluck. It showed the perfect amount of skin, highlighting her curves. To top it off, she wore a Stetson and those cowboy boots that she knew drove him wild.

The entire outfit was one giant come-hither, setting him up for the take.

"My eyes are up here," she said, the words yanking

his gaze from the tempting swell of her breasts to her lovely face.

Stifling a groan, he shook off the desire flaring through him. "You were saying."

"Do you have any interest in something real with me?"

Sex was real. And spectacular on the occasions when they'd had it, but he'd thought they had both kept things compartmentalized and delineated. Until now.

Jake squirmed in the passenger's seat of her SUV, which was parked alongside several other vehicles with parents also waiting in them to pick up their kids. The teens were inside working on a high school project or something. Becca seemed familiar with the parents and had given the obligatory wave hello when they had arrived. Not that she was a mom. She was a hard-charging, fast burner at work like him, with no time for the hassle of kids. But she was a fantastic aunt, who often pitched in to help her family when she could. Somehow, she had roped Jake into tagging along with her to pick up her nephew.

"I thought we were on the same page," Jake said. "This is just supposed to be fun. Easy. Our current arrangement works." No complications. No pressure. No expectations. No one disappointed. "If it isn't broke, don't fix it, right?" He grinned, aiming for a subtle mix of charming and honest.

His expression fell flat, failing to elicit the barest hint of a smile from her. Rolling her eyes, she sighed. He rubbed at the outline of his handy-dandy Swiss Army knife in his pocket. It had brought him luck on many occasions. He could use a little with the way this conversation was going.

Becca glanced away at the double doors of the library. "Mason hasn't responded to my text telling him that I'm here. I'll go in. See how much longer he's going to be. His Battle of the Books club should've wrapped up by now." She opened her door. "We can talk about this later."

Later?

He wanted to be done with it now. Then they could put the subject in a proverbial box, bury it and have fun, which was the point of him coming here.

Jake put a hand on her arm, stopping her. The single touch made his nerves tingle. "What's going on?"

Staying seated, she held on to the door handle. "I thought this thing with you might grow. Evolve into something real."

There was that dirty four-letter word again. He was starting to hate it.

He released a deep, weary sigh. "You don't even like me."

"I don't like how you constantly underestimate me, questioning the way I handle cases."

"In my experience, underestimating a woman, especially an attractive one who carries a badge and a gun, is a bad idea. They're usually the kind who'll ruin a man." In good ways and bad. And Becca Hammond was most certainly that kind of woman.

"You can also be a sexist jerk," she added.

"Thank you for proving my point that you don't like me," he said, and she didn't refute it, which wasn't the surprising part of this conversation.

The two of them had butted heads since they had gone through the FBI Academy together. This was not the first occasion she had called him a sexist jerk. While he was guilty of being an arrogant one at times, he certainly wasn't sexist. He respected Becca. Admired her for being one of the best. She was smart and sharp, no denying that, but she was also rash and tended to take unnecessary risks that could get her killed.

"You seemed satisfied with the way things were," he continued. "That's why I thought you called me." The last time they'd seen each other had been about two months ago. They'd had a great time, in bed, when they hadn't been fighting. "Whatever this is between us, I don't want it to change."

Their arrangement gave him a much-needed escape from the grind of his life. He'd been up-front from the beginning about what he wanted and his limitations, in the hopes to avoid this.

"I'm thirty-six," she said. "Almost thirty-seven. I like fun and easy, but I also want more."

News to him. Not once had she hinted at wanting things to get serious. "More isn't an option for me. Not right now." When they'd started hooking up, it hadn't been one for her, either.

"Figures." Heaving a breath, she hopped out of the car, slammed the door and made a beeline across the lot headed for the walkway.

Maybe they could still salvage tonight. If not, rather than letting this be a wasted trip, he'd visit his sister and her fiancé. Not that having dinner with Lynn's soon-to-be husband was his first choice. To be honest, he'd prefer to stick toothpicks in his own eyes than play nice with Nash Garner.

Jake jumped out of the SUV. "Becca, hold on a second." He hurried up beside her on the sidewalk, catching her elbow. "Are we good?"

Despite how much she got under his skin sometimes, he'd been looking forward to spending time with her.

"No." Pulling away from his grasp, Becca folded her arms, her stance turning defensive, as if she was ready for battle. "We are not *good.*"

Jake scratched his chin in bewilderment. "Since when?"

"Since I found out that I'm pregnant."

The statement hit him like a sucker punch to the solar plexus, stealing his breath.

Becca stared at him, those intelligent eyes assessing every nuance of how he was taking the news. It was impossible for him to hide his shock, even while knowing his reaction might drive a wedge between them.

His gaze dropped reflexively to her stomach. Not that he expected to see a baby bump there. "It's mine," he said, half statement, half question, a storm of emotions rolling through him.

They had decided to be exclusive, to be safe while having fun. If the situation changed, they'd agreed to discuss it. Their arrangement had made it easy for them not to risk their hearts with other people who might have expected more than sex.

He was only looking for confirmation. To hear her say it.

Becca squeezed her eyes shut, her mouth thinning

into a hard line, as though he'd uttered the worst possible thing. "Yes. It's yours."

Running a hand through his hair, he turned away, struggling to come up with the right response. He couldn't even muster a suitable facial expression.

The white van circled around again, coming into the parking lot from Seventh Street.

"Aren't you going to say anything?" Becca snapped from behind him.

The passenger door of the van flew open. A man wearing dark clothes and a dark green camo bandanna covering the lower part of his face knelt at the opening. Jake registered the barrel of a semiautomatic weapon. But it was too late.

"Get down!" he yelled right as gunfire ripped through the air. Spinning, he grabbed Becca and dove to the ground, landing on the lawn. He shielded her with his body from the rain of bullets that followed.

He listened, assessing how many might be injured or killed, how much damage was being done. But no glass shattered. No distinct pings of gunfire striking metal. Only the distant screams from the parents inside their vehicles.

The driver gunned the engine. Tires squealed. The van took off, zooming through the L-shaped parking lot around to the side of the library, headed toward Grand Avenue, where there would be plenty of pedestrians and passing cars.

"Are you all right?" Jake asked, his gaze sweeping over her in search of injuries.

Becca lay with her cheek to the grass, her eyes wide, a grimace tightening her features. "Yeah. Fine."

Jake was up on his feet, drawing his holstered weapon. Racing across the grass toward the other end of the building, he glimpsed the parking lot. None of the parents appeared hurt. Their vehicles were all undamaged. They cringed, looking frightened from the safety of their cars. The absence of visible signs of blood or calls for help left him confident there were no injuries or fatalities.

Before he rounded the corner, from his periphery he caught sight of Becca disappearing into the library.

What was she doing? She should be going back to her car to grab her cell phone and call this in.

Jake bolted through the other section of the parking lot toward Grand Avenue. If he was lucky, he might get a clear shot at one of the tires. At the very least, he'd be able to tell which direction they were headed in, when he did what Becca should be doing right now. He reached the main road as the white van screeched to a halt in front of the library.

Two armed men jumped from the van—one from the back with a duffel bag slung over his shoulder and the other from the driver's seat—leaving the van's engine running.

The men held semiautomatic weapons, the barrels raised, and pulled their triggers, sending a spray of gunfire up toward the sky as they marched up the walkway of the library.

People screamed. Children cried out. Cars braked in the street. Commotion ensued.

Jake raised his sidearm, taking aim on the assailants. "Stop! FBI!"

Both masked men glanced in his direction as a woman with salt-and-pepper hair walked out of the library. One guy seized her by the collar of her dress and shoved the muzzle of his rifle into her back.

The woman wore a name tag, but she was too far away for him to make it out. She must have been a librarian or a clerk.

Jake ached to put an end to whatever those two men were up to with a bullet in each of them, but the woman was blocking any clean shot he might take. He couldn't take the chance of hitting her or that the other guy might put a bullet in her.

Instead of firing, he said, "Drop your weapons and let her go!"

They ducked inside the library, out of his sight.

Jake dashed down the sidewalk alongside the building, headed toward the doors. He shouted at pedestrians, waving his hand at them to clear out and get a safe distance away.

At the main entrance, he tugged on one of the glass doors, but they had been chained and padlocked from the inside. The gunmen were backing away through the foyer.

The burly guy with a green camo bandanna covering his nose and mouth slipped the strap of his rifle over his shoulder, drew a 9mm from the holster on his hip and crushed the woman against him, roping an arm around her throat. He pressed the gun to her head, his finger on the trigger, and hauled her with them.

The woman stumbled, nearly falling. The guy caught her and jammed the gun even more tightly against her temple, making her flinch.

A curse slipped from Jake's mouth as she grimaced in pain. Her assailant dragged her along, using the woman as a human shield. They shoved through another set of doors, chaining those as well. Then they retreated deeper into the library until he no longer had a visual on them.

Jake swore again beneath his breath.

Becca and Mason were somewhere inside. Maybe she was able to get her nephew and the others out. But the library was large, spread over two levels. There was no telling if she had found him yet. Or if she was even aware the armed men had entered the building.

Jake took off, charging back around the library, hoping he could make it to the rear entrance before the armed men did and locked those doors, too.

At a full-blown sprint, he pushed as hard and as fast as possible, still holding his sidearm. He had to make it. He had to reach the other set of doors in time.

Too many innocent lives were on the line.

High school kids.

Unsuspecting citizens.

Becca.

He tore around the corner, his heart hammering his chest. He was barely able to breathe, but the tightness in his lungs wasn't what made him stop dead in his tracks.

The parents were out of their cars, standing in the lot, crying, staring, pointing—at a second white van that had pulled up in front of the rear entrance. Both van doors hung open. The engine left running.

A second team had entered the library.

No.

Jake raced down the walkway, heading for the back doors, knowing with each frenzied step exactly what he would find.

The rear entrance had also been chained and padlocked.

There was no way for Becca to get out. She was unarmed and trapped inside with at least four gunmen.

And she was pregnant. With his baby.

For a crazed moment, he considered shooting out the glass and storming in. He tamped the impulse down, forcing himself to stay focused. Not only would he be breaking protocol, but he would also be endangering the lives of the hostages and compromising any chance to de-escalate this volatile situation.

As a hostage negotiator, he of all people knew better.

This wasn't the time to lose it, no matter how tempted he was to do exactly that. It was bad enough that Becca was in such danger.

He pulled his cell phone and called for backup.

Chapter Two

Mason!

That was Becca's one thought. Her first instinct and only immediate concern. Ensuring her nephew was safe and would stay that way.

She'd jerked open the rear door of the library and rushed inside. She needed to get to her nephew. Have him in her sight. In her arms. She had to get him and the other kids away from the library before something else happened.

"Mason!" Scanning the main area, she ran through the first floor.

Becca shoved by confused and startled patrons. Her sixth sense was firing hot in warning, that gut feeling that had kept her alive during her twelve years with the FBI. She had no idea what had prompted the drive-by shooting, but she suspected that this was only the start of more trouble yet to come. She had ignored the warning pinging through her in the car, misguidedly believing that it had been triggered by her conversation with Jake. A sign their quasi relationship was about to end before it had even really begun.

"Mason Walker!" She darted a glance down every dense aisle lined with books that she passed. Searched the corners that had tables and seating for groups. Each second tugged at her heart, her pulse drumming in her ears. Each step she took not bringing her any closer to her nephew.

Where was he?

Worry pounded through her. Spinning around to see if she had missed him, she noticed the information desk. She ran to the man who was standing behind the counter.

His name tag read Cameron Lund.

"What's going on outside?" the librarian asked. "We heard gunshots."

"The high school Battle of the Books club," Becca said, ignoring his question. "Where are they meeting?"

"U-u-uh, upstairs. In the conference room." He pointed a shaky finger toward the staircase that was set off to the side.

It had been difficult to spot the steps from where she had entered the library.

"Call the police." She made a beeline for the stairway.

More gunfire erupted outside, bringing her to a halt. This time it had come from Grand Avenue. She spun in the direction the front entrance, but she had to peer around the bend to see it. Every muscle in her body tightened, at the ready for whatever might happen next.

Two masked gunmen barged inside the main foyer. One had a hostage at gunpoint. The other pulled out a steel chain from a duffel bag on his shoulder, looped it through the handles of the doors, and threw on a lock. As they began backing up to the second set of double doors, she pivoted for the staircase.

Mason was already on his way down the steps, along with five other teens and a teacher whom she recognized as Mr. Nolan.

Becca had to get them out of there. "Come on." She beckoned for them to hurry up.

They all hustled down the stairs, looking perplexed and scared.

Mason met her gaze. "What's happening?"

"Was that gunfire?" Mr. Nolan asked.

With no time to explain, she threw an arm around his shoulder, bringing him in close to her side. "We have to get out of here through the rear entrance. Now!"

There was no way to avoid going near the front lobby, where the gunmen were located, but if they were fast enough, they might not be seen.

Becca led them back the way she had come, keeping a firm grip on Mason. After they passed several rows of bookshelves, the information desk was in sight. Peeking around the bend once more, she glimpsed the gunmen. They had finished chaining the second set of doors and were backing up further into the library, focused on something or someone out front. But their attention wouldn't be diverted too much longer.

Right now, she and the others had a chance. They could make it.

She dashed toward the information desk along with the teens and their teacher. "Go," she said. "Get out of here. Mason, my car is in the lot. The key is in the ignition."

Mason was sixteen and a half. He'd been so eager to get his license that he had completed the requirements before he turned seventeen.

Her nephew hesitated. "What about you?"

"I'll be right behind you." If she wasn't, for whatever reason, once he made it to the car, he didn't need her to get away from there. He could drive himself. "Go. Please. Before it's too late." She waved them off toward the rear entrance and turned to Cameron Lund. "Men with guns sealed the front exit. Get out. Anyone you see on the way, tell them to go."

"Dear, God." His eyes went wide with panic. He gave her a curt nod and hurried from behind the desk.

As Cameron ran for the exit, he grabbed the arm of a coworker. Becca corralled anyone she spotted, directing them to hurry without taking the time to explain. Thankfully, it was early evening on a Thursday, off-peak hours, and she'd only come across a handful of patrons.

They had mere seconds before those men started searching for hostages.

With three others beside her, she rounded the corner of the aisle that led to the rear entrance and stopped short.

The two staff members, the other patrons, Mr. Nolan and all the kids, including Mason, were still inside.

Then she saw the reason why.

More armed men wearing bandannas had chained the doors and turned their weapons on everyone.

They were all trapped in the library with gunmen. An icy chill slid through Becca's veins. She hadn't been fast enough.

The sound of sirens pierced the air.

Footsteps followed by profanity came from behind her. The other men and the woman with cropped graying hair that they still had at gunpoint closed in. The woman wore a name tag that read Abigail Abshire.

"What are all these kids doing here?" the squat, barrel-chested man with a black paisley face mask asked, barely suppressing his alarm. "It's only supposed to be a couple of people plus the librarians."

Becca took everything in, absorbing as many details as she could process. Two of them carried AR-15s. The other two had Rugers. Each man also had a Glock G19. Standard magazine capacity was fifteen rounds. They were dressed in similar fashion. Dark cargo pants. Utility boots. Plain black T-shirts. The only difference in attire was their choice of neck gaiters that had been pulled up over their faces.

"That's what I was told," the big man, holding Abigail, said. His bandanna was dark green camo. "I don't know. Something must've happened." He shrugged.

"Why are you kids here?" asked a tall, thin man near the doors. His tone was calm, his voice steady; a gray mask covered his face.

No one responded. The teens bunched closer together. One let out a whimper as a gun was turned on them.

"Don't hurt them, please." Becca stepped forward. "They're children."

"Shut up." Paisley pointed his weapon at her, and she raised her hands in surrender. "No one asked you."

"It was a last-minute change because the high school lost power," Mr. Nolan said, his entire body shaking. "We came here to prep for our competition."

Her sister, Clare, hadn't given her the reason for the change. All Becca knew was that Mason's parents had been busy and her nephew needed to be picked up at the library after his club finished meeting. She'd been free since she'd taken a few days off and was happy to pitch in.

More sirens blared. They were much closer now. From the sound, the authorities were just outside both entrances. Beyond the rear doors, she saw flashing strobe lights.

Most likely from the sheriff's office. Their department was located further down Grand Avenue and would be faster to respond than the police.

In a matter of hours—she estimated three, possibly four—a special weapons and tactics team from Cheyenne, the next town over, would be on-site. Laramie didn't have the funding for their own specialized unit. Not that the community usually had much need for SWAT. It was rare that you heard a siren unless it was a medical emergency or a fire.

"You should let the kids go," Becca said. "Whatever you're doing here, they're not a part of your plan." That was obvious by their reaction to their presence. "You don't want to be the cause of an innocent kid being killed."

"We're not going to hurt them." The calm one, Gray, moved where she could see his eyes.

At that distance, she couldn't make out the color, but the control that stared back at her resonated clearly. He was determined to see this through. Whatever the purpose of *this* was.

"Mistakes can happen all too easily," Becca said. "For every man with a gun, the likelihood of something going wrong increases exponentially. With four of you, the odds are high that blood will be shed."

"What do you know, huh?" Paisley asked as he narrowed his beady brown eyes at her.

She didn't respond to him, keeping her attention on the other man, Gray.

"Maybe she has a point," said a guy wearing a blue bandanna. Balding, with deep wrinkles set in his forehead, he appeared much older than his cohorts, from what she could tell. He and Gray exchanged a pointed look. "One of them might get hurt. Accidents happen. This isn't what we discussed. We wanted to keep the number of hostages manageable. No children if possible. Let's not lose sight of why we're here. Of what we're fighting for. We don't need a bunch of hormonal teenagers to deal with, too."

"Why take the risk in keeping them?" Becca asked, taking advantage of the opening Blue had given her. "It's not worth it. Why not just let them go, now, before things get more out of hand?"

They didn't need to endanger children. There were enough adults to use as bargaining chips.

Gray looked at the kids, hopefully considering the

validity of their points. He stepped closer, zeroing in on a boy with blond curls. "I recognize you." Then his gaze slid over a girl standing beside him. "You, too. What are your last names?"

"Schroeder," the blond boy said.

"Pietsch," the girl answered.

Becca stiffened. The surnames were familiar. She knew their parents all too well from working the assignment that had brought her to Laramie as a part of the FBI's joint task force.

Blue shook his head. "Damn it."

"But this is good," Paisley said, looking at Gray. "Right?"

"It might be." Gray nodded. "The presence of the mayor's son and Councilwoman Pietsch's daughter could work to our advantage," he said, composed and calculating. "This wasn't the way we had planned it, but this coincidence will give us more leverage. And we're going to need all that we can get."

That was the man calling the shots.

"Why are you doing this?" Becca asked. "What do you want?" The sooner their motive was revealed, the sooner this might be resolved. What could they possibly hope to gain by taking hostages in a library? "If you told me, I might be able to help you figure out a better way of getting it."

"Shut. Up." Paisley, who had the gun pointed at her with a shaky hand, stepped far too close and pressed the muzzle to her forehead. "I don't like mouthy women who don't know how to listen. Do you understand me?"

Becca's stomach churned with dread, stilling her. In

the blink of an eye, he could pull the trigger and end her life and that of her unborn child. Not once on the job had she experienced such helplessness, been paralyzed by fear. But she wasn't afraid for herself. She feared for Mason, the other children and the one growing inside her. The baby she never thought she wanted or was ready for until she had watched the positive sign pop up on the home pregnancy test a week ago.

Someone she loved already and would do anything to protect.

Convinced that Paisley would have no qualms about shooting her, Becca zipped her lips.

"No!" Her nephew's voice drew everyone's attention. "Leave her alone. You better not hurt her, because she's—"

"Stop, Mason," Becca said, cutting him off. "Don't."

She suspected he was about to expose her as an FBI agent. That was the last thing she wanted. The gunmen would most likely shoot her, leaving Mason and the other hostages to fend for themselves. She needed to bide her time and strike when she had the chance.

"Because she's what?" Gray asked.

Mason looked to her, and she shook her head, telling him to remain silent.

"Speak up, boy," Paisley demanded.

Tension swelled. They weren't going to drop it. Not till they got an answer.

"Because I'm pregnant." The words flew out of her mouth. It was the best thing she could think of to appease them. "My nephew was worried. We all just want to get out of this alive and unharmed."

"Then do as you're told," Paisley said, "and keep your mouth shut."

She nodded to the gunman that she would be quiet.

For now. Until she could speak to the leader when Paisley, who had a problem with her, wasn't within earshot.

"Are we agreed that we keep them?" Gray asked.

Paisley and Camo both nodded.

Blue shuffled his feet, hesitating a moment. Then he looked at Gray. "Agreed. If you think this is the right call, then I trust you."

"Good. We push forward with the plan." Gray glanced at a wristwatch. "It's five thirty-five. Mark it, guys. SWAT will be here in three hours," he said, and she wondered how they knew the response time, including how long for a unit to mobilize and travel to Laramie. "Move the kids to the story time room." He pointed to Paisley.

The stocky guy lowered the muzzle from her head and ushered the kids away down the corridor. As they passed, she met Mason's glance. In that one look, she did her best to reassure him that she would do everything in her power to keep him safe.

Gray looked over the rest of them, eight more hostages. Finally, he picked four and gestured to Blue and Camo. "Put two in front of each set of doors. Zip-tie them to chairs before SWAT gets here and puts sharpshooters in place. Be sure to take their cell phones. If the police decide to breach without meeting our demands, I want them to see their faces and think long and hard if the collateral damage is worth it. Then one of you stand guard at the front and rear but stay out of the line of sight of the doors and windows."

This had been well planned, but she didn't think that they were hard-core professionals. Not with the shaky gun-hand, the outright questioning of how to proceed once something unexpected happened, and the need to tell his men to stay out of sight of snipers.

"The rest of you," Gray said, gesturing to Becca and the other hostages, "are going to the story time room. You, Lund, lead the way. Walk single file." Slinging the strap of his rifle over his shoulder, he took out the 9mm, pressed his gun to the back of Abigail Abshire's head and brought up the rear.

Becca walked in between Nolan and Abigail. She would've preferred to have been in Abigail's place. Closer to Gray, so that they could talk. If she could build a rapport with him, maybe even Blue, eventually one of them would lower their guard. Then she would act. Disarm him if possible and shift the power dynamic.

She had two things that these men seemed to lack: training and experience. Under the right circumstances, it might be enough to give her the upper hand.

If she understood what they were after, it would help. None of their actions thus far revealed their motive. What was the point of all this?

Through the large glass window of the story time room, she saw the kids seated on the carpet. The walls were decorated with fanciful trees, colorful animals and letters painted with a whimsical flare. It was a good spot to put the hostages. The room was across from the information desk and could be seen from several angles, allowing the gunmen to easily keep an eye on them, and there were no outside windows. No way to escape.

At the doorway, Lund entered first and the rest of them followed.

"Go sit with the others," Gray instructed.

Becca went to Mason and sat cross-legged between him and Pietsch's daughter. She wrapped her arm around her nephew and held him close.

"If you have a cell phone on you," Gray said, "take it out and hand it over. Failure to do so and we find it will result in severe consequences."

Paisley opened his duffel, took out a smaller vinyl bag and started collecting them.

Mason removed his backpack, unzipped it and took his out. As Pietsch's daughter pulled a phone out from the back pocket of her jeans, Becca noticed that no one else was paying attention to the girl. The other two men were focused on Nolan, who was having trouble unzipping his messenger bag.

Becca slipped her hand on top of the girl's, covering the phone. The teen met her eyes, an anxious expression tightening over her young face. But Becca put a finger to her mouth, urging the girl to stay quiet. She flicked a glance around the room at the others. While no one was looking, she slid the cell phone away a few inches and slipped it inside her boot. The girl quickly straightened, facing forward.

Paisley stepped in front of them with the bag held out. Lowering her gaze, Becca avoided eye contact with the man, playing the part of cooperative captive, not wanting to agitate him.

Mason dropped his cell phone inside the bag.

"Where are the keys to these rooms?" Gray asked.

Oh no. They were going to lock them in.

Lund said nothing as he cringed, looking like he wanted to disappear into the wall.

"The information desk," Abigail said. "Top right-hand drawer."

Gray gestured for Paisley to go. The other man hustled out of the room. Holding his Glock, Gray looked them over, his eyes giving nothing away. It didn't take long for the stocky guy to return with a set of keys jangling in his hand.

"Stay calm," Gray said. "Keep quiet. Hopefully, this will be over tonight."

Paisley snorted. "Don't bet on it."

A cell phone rang, echoing in the small room.

Becca's pulse spiked, her mind leaping to the worst—that she was caught. Then she realized the sound wasn't coming from the phone she had hidden.

Gray pulled one from his pocket and looked at the screen. "Check every aisle and upstairs to make sure no one else is here," Gray said to the other guy, and the two men left the room, shutting the door behind them.

As Paisley locked the door, Becca leaned in close to the girl. "What's your passcode?" she whispered in her ear. "I need to silence your phone."

"One-two-three-four," she said, keeping her voice low so only she could hear, and Becca hated that the teenager didn't have better password security. "I turned off the ringer and notifications before the book club met."

Relief whispered through Becca as she nodded to her.

That was good. She wouldn't have to risk exposing the phone prematurely to take care of it. Now she had to wait for the right opportunity to contact Jake. She only hoped that by the time that happened, she had more information to give him. Something, anything that would help bring this situation to a bloodless end.

Standing in front of the glass window, Gray answered the ringing phone. "Yeah, we did it. We're inside," he said, his voice carrying loud enough to be overheard in the story room. "Let us know once it hits the news. National." Gray began walking away toward the information desk. "Everything went almost exactly like you planned."

You planned?

Who was the mastermind, and what on earth did they hope to achieve?

"WHAT DO YOU mean almost?" his goddaughter asked. "What went wrong? Is anybody hurt?"

"No, no," Frank said. "Everyone is fine. It's just that there are some kids here from the local high school."

There was always the chance that kids might be present. It was a public library after all. But for weeks they had monitored peak and off-peak hours, which times of day were more likely to have small children or teenagers. They'd narrowed it down to the best window of opportunity. Still, no plan was perfect, regardless of how meticulous his goddaughter had been.

"What do you want to do about them?" she asked. "Let them go?"

They had discussed contingencies and brainstormed

how to deal with them. The first option had been to release them, but this was a one-in-a-thousand opportunity he couldn't resist.

"No," he said. "We're going to hang on to them."
Keeping his back to the story time room, he pulled the
neck gaiter down from his face. "Turns out we've got
the mayor's son and Pietsch's daughter." Dumb luck.
Perhaps even Providence. Who was he to reject a gift
from the universe? His gut told him this was the best
course of action. "It'll intensify the pressure."

Silence. His goddaughter, Hannah, was rarely
speechless.

He could tell she was thinking, measuring her words
carefully. That beautiful mind of hers was what made
her such a crackerjack hacker and a brilliant strategist
who had led them down this path. Their last resort.

Finally, Hannah said, "It could also backfire. If we
lose in the court of public opinion, we'll never get what
we want."

"We've got to win the public over first. Once the
world knows why we're doing this, understands what
we're fighting for, I think we can do it." Still, he sighed,
not wanting to admit that she was also right. This was
a deadly game of chance where more than lives were at
stake. They were all so desperate for this to work. "This
won't backfire so long as none of the kids, especially
those two, don't get hurt," he said. "We'll keep them
contained and make sure nothing happens to them."

If he had to use an adult hostage to make a point, he
wouldn't hesitate to do so.

"Can you do this?" she asked.

"I'll see it through." Determination burned hot as hellfire through him. He and the others had waited so long for this. Their time had come. "Whatever it takes."

"The cops will try to strike a deal, but there's no way to know if all parties will hold up their end of the bargain."

"That's why I wanted the kids. Pietsch and Schroeder will dial up the pressure to have our demands met. We might not have to go to the next level." Frank didn't want this to get bloody. None of them did, because instead of bringing down a bad guy, they would become the bad guys. But if blood needed to be shed to achieve their ultimate goal, then so be it.

Glancing back at the story time room, Frank knew exactly who he would start with.

"Even if *he* agrees, I don't trust him to keep his word," Hannah said. "The bastard is rotten to the core."

Frank couldn't agree more. None of them trusted *him*. Or the system. "We'll see how it plays out. But if things don't go according to plan, if the worst happens—"

"Don't say that." Her concern resonated over the phone. "This will work. It has to."

Frank loved her more than he could say. She was the daughter he never had. "But if it doesn't," he said, "and something goes wrong…" They could all be shot and killed. A possibility they had planned for and a risk they were prepared to accept. Not that their lives mattered. Survival wasn't their endgame.

It was too late for that.

"I know," Hannah said, her voice like steel. "I'm ready. I only hope that it doesn't come to that."

"Just remember that any blood spilled is *his* fault. Not ours."

"Justice for one," she said, "justice for all."

"Justice for all." That was the goal.

But deep down he was really doing this for only one person.

His sweet Marianne.

Chapter Three

As an FBI hostage negotiator, Jake was used to traveling with little notice. While in transit to a crisis situation, his routine was to mentally prepare, use the time to examine the details of the case, the layout of the building, learn what he could about the kidnappers if their identity was known. There was a process, steps to follow when dealing with a hostage taker. Still, he relied on his instinct to guide him.

But this was the first time ever that he'd been tossed into the fire with no warning.

Or, rather, had voluntarily jumped in. He couldn't allow another negotiator to handle this. Not when fate had brought him here, at this moment. Not when Becca was trapped inside.

Getting her and the other hostages out of this alive demanded his undivided attention.

Jake didn't have his usual team, but he was surrounded by some of the finest law enforcement had to offer from Becca's joint task force. She had shared details with him about her team and their assignment in Laramie, so he was aware of their skill set.

In less than an hour, they had set up a white tent in the parking lot of the library, adjacent to the brick wall that had no windows, to serve as their center of operations. It was a temporary solution until the mobile command center arrived. Because Becca was a federal employee and among the hostages being held, the FBI was able to step in. They pooled their resources with the deputies under Sheriff Daniel Clark, who would handle all the updates with the media while the FBI took the operational lead.

"It's fortunate that you're here," Sheriff Clark said to him. "There was a hostage negotiator coming with SWAT from Cheyenne. Once they learned you were here, they decided to keep him back. He's new to the position. He's got thirty-two hours of classroom training and role play with uniformed staff, but he's never been involved in a real hostage incident. Besides, his wife's in labor. But the unit won't be here for at least two more hours. That's precious time we won't have to waste with you handling it, Special Agent Delgado."

"He has a stellar reputation as the best in the region," Nash said, giving Jake a rare compliment. "They call him the miracle worker. If anybody can end this with none of the hostages getting hurt or worse, it's him."

They had both been working on cutting each other some slack after the engagement, for Lynn's sake. They were going to be family. Although Jake would resolve this hostage situation no matter what—not only for Becca but also for every other person being held captive—he recognized that Nash hadn't needed to give such high praise.

Perhaps he needed to try a little harder with Nash.

Clapping a hand on his future brother-in-law's shoulder, Jake gave him a slight nod of appreciation for the support. "High-risk negotiation is my specialty, but we've got one of our own inside and six minors, which raises the stakes considerably."

"That's an understatement. We're talking about a councilwoman's daughter and the mayor's son," Rocco Sharp said. With his goatee, scruffy hair, tattoos and muscular build, he had an imposing appearance. He was the sole Alcohol, Tobacco and Firearms agent on the interagency task force. According to Becca, before Rocco had joined the team, he had enhanced his tactical ATF skills by working on an elite rapid response team for several years. At a moment's notice he had deployed across the country to handle high-risk situations from mass shootings to hostage crises.

Jake couldn't have handpicked a better agent to have at his side, helping get this resolved.

"The parents who weren't already present, waiting to pick up their kid when the gunmen arrived, have been notified," Detective Brian Bradshaw said. Assigned to the task force from the local police department, he was former military and supposedly possessed skills that made him an asset. "That was the Schroeder family, Felicia Pietsch and the Walkers."

Becca's family.

Silence fell between them as they exchanged glances. With each second that ticked by, the tension in the tent only increased.

Becca's sister, Clare, and her brother-in-law, Tim

Walker, were on site. Nash had spoken with them when they arrived.

Under such horrendous circumstances wasn't how Jake had thought he'd meet Becca's family. Not that he had seriously considered the possibility.

He hadn't been able to bring himself to go over and speak with them. Not until he got their son and Becca out of there safely. Or, at a minimum, he could assure them that neither had been harmed.

A commotion outside in the parking lot drew their attention.

"It's the mayor and councilwoman." Brian gestured at the two emotional individuals yelling at some deputies who were preventing them from entering the tent.

"I'll go talk to them," the sheriff offered as he put on his Stetson, "and do what I can to calm them down."

Farther back on the sidewalk, reporters and a flock of onlookers had gathered alongside the first responder vehicles.

"Can you also do something about the crowd?" Jake asked Clark. "The number of lookie-loos in the area keeps growing." This was an active crime scene, not a spectator sport. The last thing they needed to do was give the kidnappers additional targets. If those gunmen decided to smash out a window and open fire, any of those civilians would be close enough to take a stray bullet. Then they'd have pandemonium and a possible bloodbath on their hands.

"I've already spoken to one of my deputies about it and she's working on it. Try to understand that something of this magnitude doesn't usually happen around here and folks are used to this," Clark said. "We're a small, tight-knit community. The odds are high those bystanders probably know one or more of the hostages inside. They're not out there because they're simply curious. They're *concerned*." He strode out of the tent and made his way over to the burgeoning disorder.

The other parents were gathering behind Schroeder and Pietsch—with the exception of the Walkers—their fear and anger visibly bubbling over as the sheriff approached them.

Jake didn't envy the sheriff the difficult position he was in. Jake never dealt with the family members of the hostages. It was too draining. Too much of a distraction that would split his focus.

The current conditions for him to work under were already far from ideal. This was personal, but he had to figure out a way not to let emotion dictate his actions. Not that he was quite sure how he felt about the bombshell Becca had dropped on him.

Pregnant.

With his baby.

It was still surreal. He couldn't wrap his head around it, much less come to terms with it.

The first time they had been together had occurred while he had been visiting his sister after she'd been through a life-and-death situation in which Nash had saved her. Jake had bumped into Becca at his Aunt's bar and grill, Delgado's. They'd had a heated argument, but they had made amends over drinks.

Alcohol had obliterated their inhibitions. Sparks had flown. They had ended up in bed at her place. In the morning, in the sober light of day, the conversation had been all about work. They had discussed their respective cases, like colleagues. No lovey-dovey chitchat. No kisses goodbye. The next time he had gone up to specifically to see her, he'd called her from Delgado's. Played it cool. Invited her for dinner, but they had never made it past the second round of cocktails. That's when they'd talked about how their arrangement would work. The whole weekend and the others after they hadn't been able to keep their hands off each other.

He loved sparring with her as much as he enjoyed sleeping with her.

Jake couldn't forget any of those nights over the past few weeks, no matter how much he had tried. Logically, he knew he never should have touched her. Kissed her. Slept with her. But perhaps he hadn't really tried all that hard to erase the memories, since he had kept going back for more.

Never before had he been like that with another woman. Consumed with desire. Drunk from the pleasure.

And look at where the mistake of losing his head had gotten them both.

When that van door had opened and he'd seen the gun, he hadn't been thinking about the pregnancy as he shoved Becca to the ground. She had landed facedown on her stomach.

Could that have hurt the baby?

His instinct had been to protect her.

An image of Becca racing into the library slid into

his head. He clenched his hand at his side. He didn't even know if she was okay in there.

Should he have tried to take the shot at the gunmen when he'd had them in his sights? If he had, they never would have sealed off the Grand Avenue entrance. But that would have meant risking the life of the first hostage they'd taken.

Jake had learned she was Abigail Hayes Abshire. A sixty-six-year-old widow. A mother of three and grandmother of five, who had decided to go back to work after retirement to clerk at the library. He shoved away the thought of Abigail with the gun pressed to her head. Of Becca and wondering if she was all right.

Regardless of any personal connection, he had a job to do and intended to get everyone being held out of this alive and well.

"Any idea what these guys are after?" Brian asked.

"None whatsoever." Jake wished like hell that he knew what their motive was, wished he knew who they were. Then he could get a detailed profile on them that would allow him to get inside their heads. There was also one question he had yet to voice to the others. Out of all the places they could have invaded and taken hostages, why had they chosen a library?

"Maybe they're going to try to ransom Schroeder and Pietsch's kids," Rocco said.

Jake shook his head. "I highly doubt that's the reason why they invaded the library."

"How can you be so sure?" Rocco countered.

"Because those kids weren't supposed to be there. It was a last-minute change. Whatever the gunmen's reasons, it's something else." Jake looked over his notes. "We need more information." Ideally before he initiated contact, but he had pushed it for as long as he dared. The hostage takers had been inside two hours. Jake's patience was one of his strengths. It was better to get things done right rather than fast. No two incidents were ever alike, so there were no "tried-and-true" techniques. He had to be ready for anything and trust in his extensive training.

"I'm going to check with forensics," Rocco said, "and see if they have come up with anything on their search of the vans that would get us one step closer to identifying the assailants."

They'd already run the license plates and learned that they'd been lifted from two sedans that reported the plates as stolen earlier that day. The gunmen had been wearing gloves, but sometimes people got sloppy and messed up. In the event they got lucky and pulled a clean print, they might get a hit on it.

Brian stepped around the table. "With the sheriff's department short-staffed and stretched thin managing the environment around the library, I've tapped Laramie PD resources. Since you said that one or both of the white vans circled the library before the gunmen stormed in, they're checking traffic cam footage. They'll also backtrack where the vans came from as far as possible. Maybe we can get an image of the drivers' faces unmasked. But you should know that we don't have many cameras, and the farther out from the center of town, the less coverage there is. As soon as we get anything, we'll let you know."

With the low population and condensed town center, having few traffic cameras made sense, but it was also one of the biggest disadvantages.

As soon as Rocco and Brian left the tent, Nash turned to him. "Can we talk bluntly for a minute, no sugarcoating things?"

Suppressing a groan, Jake realized that Nash's supportive act had been too good to be true. There was a catch. *And here it comes.* "I've never had a problem speaking my mind with you. So, what's up?"

"Is there something going on between you and Becca?" When Jake stiffened, he held up a palm. "Hold on." Nash paused, his steely gaze narrowing, and Jake felt the frost radiating from him. "You've been to Laramie a few times recently and it hasn't been for official business with the task force, and it hasn't been to see Lynn or your aunt. She checked the visitor log at the senior living center."

Their Aunt Miriam had dementia. Her declining health was the reason Lynn relocated there from Colorado to help manage Delgado's bar and grill and to get their aunt settled in a facility. Although Miriam no longer remembered him, he usually visited her with his sister.

"What's your point?" Jake asked.

"Lynn said that you don't have any friends here and that you've always hated this town."

The only friends he'd ever had there were his cousins, Dean and Lucas. After his uncle died and his aunt remarried, she isolated herself from the rest of the family and sent her sons to Colorado for summer visits. Jake had found it a relief that he didn't have to go back to Laramie. Now, Dean and Lucas were in the CIA. The only reason Jake had started coming back to this town was because of Lynn.

"Your sister didn't even know you were here now until I told her what was happening. I'm only asking about you and Becca because I need to know if this is personal for you."

Jake's professional duty always came first.

Always.

It was the reason he no longer tried having a relationship after his divorce years ago. His ex-wife, Sam, had told him the strain of his work had been too much. Their marriage had barely lasted eighteen months before she'd had enough and punched out regardless that he hadn't wanted a divorce. All because his job had been his priority instead of her.

He could shove sentimentality aside, his fear and worry about Becca and not knowing if she was all right.

Negotiating couldn't be about the negotiator's feelings. The moment emotions influenced decisions, it became more dangerous for the hostages. No one understood that better than him.

He wasn't going to compromise this case, but he also wasn't going to walk away from it. "Are you asking as the supervisory agent of the task force?" Jake asked. "Or as my future brother-in-law?"

Folding his arms, Nash tipped his head to the side. "Both." The frost in his gray eyes turned glacial.

Jake didn't understand what his sister saw in this guy. Sure, he was tall and buff and she probably found him wildly attractive, but he was never what Jake would describe as warm or friendly or even pleasant.

"Isn't it a little late to be asking me now?" Jake asked. "You've already vouched for me. This is a done deal."

"Nothing is set in stone."

Nothing but Nash's personality.

"The SWAT negotiator is greener than the grass outside and is no longer prepping to mobilize," Jake pointed out. "We don't have time to waste waiting on an alternate who isn't as good as I am. You need the best on this." He wasn't being arrogant, only honest.

"What I need is to hear the truth from you. Because if this goes sideways, it's my career on the line. Give it to me straight. Is there a conflict of interest here?"

Jake took the FBI's motto to heart and prided himself on his *fidelity*, *bravery* and *integrity*. He always operated aboveboard. Not once had he lied to a fellow agent, much less one whom he was about to be related to. But he considered it. For a split second.

"Becca and I are…" What was the word for it? A multitude of mixed emotions welled in his chest, but he tamped them down. "We're involved." He wasn't going to toss his integrity out the window. He also wasn't going to allow Nash the chance to give him a hard time about negotiating this hostage situation due to his conflict of interest, so he continued, "If this goes sideways, it is my career. Not yours. I'll take the hit. But I have to do this. You can't pull me from this detail. No one else has to know that you're aware of my personal connection to Becca."

"I don't lie. Ever."

Something they had in common and at least one thing Jake liked about the guy. "Nothing, and no one, is going to stop me from heading up this case."

Nash nodded. "You won't get any resistance from me. I just need to know what I'm signing up for."

What? Jake doubted his hearing. "You're willing to back me on this? Why?"

"If it were Lynn in there, I'd feel the same as you do. Besides, everything that I said to the sheriff and the rest of the team about your skills as a hostage negotiator was true."

"You've got that much confidence in me that you'd risk your career?"

"Your track record may speak for itself, but I have no clue if your personal involvement will limit your effectiveness here," Nash said matter-of-factly. "So, no. I have my doubts. But Lynn doesn't. She believes in you."

His sister wouldn't let bias color her judgment. She was a psychotherapist who read people for a living. She knew that Jake would never let anything get in the way of him doing his job.

"If you haven't noticed by now, I would do absolutely anything for Lola," Nash said, using the family nickname for his sister, and something about it softened Jake a little. "That includes trusting you and treating you as a brother. An estranged brother I don't get along with, but still family."

Jake respected Nash's stone-cold honesty as well as his loyalty. This was big for Nash to go out on a limb like this. He wouldn't let him or Becca down.

"The feeling is mutual." Jake took a breath, relieved that he would be able to see this through. "If it'll put your mind at ease about the way I handle operations, I don't negotiate alone. It's standard for me to have a partner. Someone who can hear everything along with me and listen between the lines while I concentrate on calming the kidnapper down and validating and acknowledging their needs." Also, it was good for him to bounce his ideas off other smart people. "You'd be perfect."

For all Nash's faults, he was a shrewd agent, and his input would be invaluable.

"You've got it. So, what's the next step?" Nash asked.

"I open a line of communication with the kidnappers." They'd had the library's public phone lines shut down, but Jake had kept a private extension open to use. He'd been assured that the call would go through to the information desk. "Let's find out what they want."

"It's about time," Mayor William Schroeder said, storming into the tent with Councilwoman Pietsch and Sheriff Clark right on his heels. He was younger than Jake had expected, not much older than himself. Early forties at the most. With his suit and tie, his blond curly hair cropped close around the sides and classic features, he could be a poster boy for politicians. "Why haven't you already reached out to those madmen to see what on earth they want?"

This was the last thing Jake needed. He wished he had the mobile command center already that had a door that locked. It was on the way from the closest field office, which happened to be his, located in Denver.

"I want a better explanation about your process. What's the reason behind the delay?" Schroeder's hard blue gaze bounced between Jake and Nash. "I spoke with the head of my security team about this. He informed me that every hour that goes by, there's a greater chance of something going wrong. Those kidnappers might panic because they're surrounded and react badly. This needs to end. Quickly. You should have already made contact," he said, jabbing a finger in Jake's direction, "found out what they want and have formulated a plan to rush in and rescue our kids."

"That's right," Pietsch said, standing beside the mayor. Her dark hair was pulled back in a tight bun and in her light brown eyes swam a sea of emotions.

These tense personal encounters—the raw, tortured emotions pouring out at him—Jake avoided like the plague. He could imagine how difficult this must be for them, but his only obligation was to the hostages. Being a great negotiator meant being the calm in the storm. The guiding light at the end of a dark tunnel.

Drawing himself up to his full six feet, he tilted his chin up. "Rushing is what gets people killed," he said. "Whether it's in making contact or breaching a building. Calculated action, patience and control is what's required." That last part above all, staying in control, was what he needed if he had any hope of helping anyone. "I've got a lot of experience doing this—"

"That may be," Schroeder said, cutting him off, "but I'm not satisfied with the way things are being handled thus far. My head of security is on his way over. He's a private contractor with extensive experience. His name is Leonard Guidry," Schroeder said, and the name rang a vague bell in Jake's head, but he couldn't pinpoint why. "He'll be a part of this team going forward and will be apprised of all pertinent details."

"Just a minute," Nash said. "I didn't agree to that."

"No, but I did." Clark stepped forward. "Remember, your task force and you, Special Agent Delgado, are working in concert with the sheriff's department, and I appreciate the assistance. Mr. Guidry will only act as a consultant, if needed. He will have zero authority. If he gets in the away or obstructs you from carrying out your duties, he will be removed from the command post. Is that agreeable to everyone?" Clark asked, looking around.

Pietsch was the first to nod.

"Yes," said the mayor. "That works for me."

Nash slid a glance at Jake before responding. "We'll see how it goes."

That was sufficient for Schroeder and Pietsch to stalk out of the tent.

Jake had worked with consultants in the past for various reasons, but he'd never had one thrust upon him to serve as someone else's eyes and ears. An unnecessary complication. Things would go much smoother if this Guidry character wasn't involved. "Why did you cave to his demand?" he asked the sheriff. "Do you have any idea how much harder this is going to make things?" He was already in a pressure cooker and didn't need the heat turned any higher from those who should be trying to help him.

Clark put his hands on his hips. "When this is over,

I still have to live and work here, while you get to go back to Denver. I'd like more than one term as sheriff. I'm not proud to admit it, but Schroeder's support would be good when my election rolls around. I don't know Guidry. The mayor did rattle off an impressive list of credentials. He sounds more than qualified. We all want the same thing. To save the hostages. Like I said, if Guidry turns out to be more of a hindrance than a help, I won't stand in your way of getting rid of him. In fact, I'll give him the heave ho myself."

"Even if it costs you Schroeder's support come election time?" Jake asked, needing to know if they could count on the sheriff.

"I like my job. I'm good at it, too. But I would never jeopardize a life to keep it. I'm here to serve and protect. That's all."

"In a situation like this, we need one person making the decisions," Jake said. "A single touchstone, and that's me. No more surprises that could affect the outcome of things. Okay?"

"All right," Clark said in agreement.

The sound of Schroeder speaking to someone outside the tent had Clark looking over his shoulder. "Speak of the devil. Guidry's here. I'll go grease the wheels and explain the rules to him before he comes in." The sheriff headed out.

"Hey," Nash said to Jake. "In a town like this, the mayor carries more weight than you'd expect. Daniel is dealing with two 'firsts' as sheriff. The first to be appointed rather than elected because the last one was corrupt. He's also the first Black sheriff. He feels like he has a lot to prove, and recently he's learned the hard way how political his position can be. He abhors playing the game, but I guess he has to. From what I've seen, he's a great sheriff. Let's not judge him too harshly on this call. Okay?"

It was difficult not to, but technically, Jake was the outsider, so he would try. Clark didn't have any issue when it came to relinquishing operational control of the situation to Jake and the task force. He seemed a reasonable man interested in doing the right thing. Jake just didn't want personality differences, especially from needless personnel, mucking things up.

"We've all got the same goal," Jake said. "Perhaps it'll be fine."

As someone entered the tent, they both turned.

A tall, lean, dark-haired man strode up to table. He seemed out of place wearing a T-shirt and jeans, considering he was the mayor's head of security and was aware of the situation. "Which one of you is Special Agent Delgado?"

"I'm Jake Delgado," Jake said, holding his hand out. "I presume you're Leonard Guidry."

"Leo," he said with a neutral smile, not taking his hand.

Jake bristled at his rudeness while at the same time feeling ridiculous for extending his hand in the first place. But then he quickly realized that was the point. This private contractor was someone who wanted his counterparts off-kilter from the start. Jake looked him over, sizing him up.

This man was not here to be a team player. Whatever

his intention, maybe try to seize control of the situation somehow, Jake didn't trust him. As soon as he got the chance, he'd have someone get a copy of Leo's supposed credentials and do a little digging.

"I'm Supervisory Special Agent Garner," Nash said. "You understand you're not to get in the way, right?"

"My role is to observe, advise and watch out for the interests of the hostages," Leo said in a level, detached voice. "I was told you're ready to make contact with the kidnappers. I think you should stop twiddling your thumbs and get to it. Enough time has been squandered."

Sooner or later, Leo Guidry was definitely going to be a problem.

Jake was betting that it would be sooner.

Chapter Four

"What's going to happen to us?" Mason asked.

Becca wished she knew for certain. They had been trapped inside the library for more than two hours, but she had faith in the law enforcement working to get them released. She put her arm around her nephew, bringing him closer so he could rest his head on her shoulder. "We're going to get through this. It'll take some time, but you and your friends are going to walk out of this building and into your parents' arms."

"How do you know?" he asked.

"Because beyond these walls, there's the sheriff's department and the combined power of the joint task force." The FBI. The Laramie Police Department. The ATF.

And there was also Jake.

Despite their personal complications, she knew he was an excellent hostage negotiator. How ironic that many of the traits that made him so great at his job were also the same ones preventing them from evolving beyond casual sex into something real. It was so easy for him to compartmentalize everything while blocking out his feelings.

The whole time she had been falling for him. Harder and harder every time they had slept together.

Even though he could annoy and frustrate her like no other, she'd found herself cuddling with him, melting into him, stealing soft embraces. Before long, she was focusing more on the things she appreciated about him. His strength. His confidence, which was borderline arrogance, but was also sexy. His honesty—an admirable quality that was so hard to find.

She might not always like what he had to say, but she could count on it to be sincere.

Becca recalled the things he'd said to her in the car.

This is just supposed to be fun. Easy. Our current arrangement works.

Whatever this is between us, I don't want it to change.

More isn't an option for me.

While she had been falling in love, he had continued to disconnect from his feelings. The entire time it had just been sex for him.

But right now, it was a comfort that he could block his emotions and live for a mission like this. If anyone could talk these guys down without losing control, it was him.

Sometimes kidnappers weren't willing to surrender, but Jake had faced that, too, and still brought out hostages alive. He hadn't lost one yet.

Yet.

The word rang in her head. There was a first time for everything.

A chill ran through her. She quickly shook off the doubt.

Becca pressed a hand to her belly. She wasn't sure how she'd felt when she had read the positive test result.

Every time she had reached for the phone to tell Jake, fear had stopped her. Fear that he would bail. Fear that he might not come back to Laramie, at least not to see her. Fear that they might not be together again, even if it was one last time.

Her brilliant plan had been to seduce him. Then tell him, face-to-face, while they were still in bed, basking in the afterglow.

Not to spit the news out after questioning him, like him not wanting a relationship was a federal offense.

She had yet to get used to the idea that she was going to be a mother.

A single mother.

They shared an intense chemistry that she had hoped could grow into something deeper for him. Whenever she was in his arms, she could see having so much more with him. But Jake had no interest in being a father, or a husband, and that was fine.

She was capable of doing this on her own.

Even if he did want this, the two of them as a couple—the three of them as a family—would probably be a disaster.

Either way, she hoped to see him again. To discuss it. To carry their child to term and deliver the baby they'd made together.

She would do everything in her power to make that happen.

One of the gunmen passed by the room. With his rifle slung over his shoulder, Paisley slowed a bit, looking in on them through the large window, and kept going.

"What if there's a shootout?" the girl beside Becca asked. She was the spitting image of Felicia Pietsch. Only younger and sweeter, not yet hardened by life.

Although being held hostage was a surefire way for these teenagers to lose some of their innocence.

"What's your name, honey?" Becca asked.

"Paige," she said, her voice low and shaky.

"If there's gunfire, don't run," Becca said. "I want you to drop to the ground." She looked at the other kids nearby. "That goes for all of you. Stay low. Do you understand?"

The teens nodded. Paige brought her knees up to her chest, wrapping her arms around her legs, and began to rock.

"Tell that to the hostages they've strapped to chairs in front of the doors," Nolan said. "They can't drop to the ground. They wouldn't stand a chance. They'll be as good as Swiss cheese."

Some of the kids cringed. One girl with light brown hair started to cry.

"This isn't helpful," Becca said to him. "We need to try to keep them calm."

Nolan rubbed the heel of his palm against his forehead. "Fairy tales aren't helpful, either. Let's see how you feel when they rotate us and we're the ones strapped to a chair, being used as a deterrent to prevent the police from entering."

It was a possibility. One she'd rather not consider. But she would cross that bridge if and when she came to it.

"As long as the cops don't force their way inside, maybe no one will get hurt," Abigail said to the girl who was in tears, patting her hand.

"We'll get through this," Becca said. "The authorities won't do anything to endanger us."

"What about those men?" Paige asked, flicking a glance up at the window. "They might do something even crazier than locking us in this building. What if they shoot us?"

Those men hadn't hurt anyone thus far. So at least a senseless massacre wasn't their goal. They were after something. Shooting hostages didn't seem like the first strategy they would employ. Not that it couldn't be their last.

"Trust me," Becca said, "the authorities are already taking this very seriously. Those men will try to avoid hurting any of us. It'll make it easier for them to negotiate if none of us are harmed."

"How long do you think we'll be in here?" Mason asked.

"I don't know." Becca rubbed her nephew's arm. "Hopefully not too long."

A phone rang out in the main area. The ring tone was different from Gray's cell and much louder.

Cameron Lund lifted his head from his knees, perking up from the corner he was huddled in. "That's the library's phone line," he said, pushing his glasses up the bridge of his nose.

Becca rose onto her knees for a better look.

Gray and Paisley converged on the information desk. They looked at the phone and then at each other.

"I'll be right back," Becca said. Staying low, she crept across the room to the glass window. The cell phone tucked in her boot rocked against her calf with each step.

"I don't think you should be doing that," Abigail said, worry deepening the wrinkles across her face. "You're going to make them angry."

Becca gestured for her to be quiet. "It's okay. I know what I'm doing." Turning back, she peeked through the window.

The two men were turned toward the phone with their profiles to her. The had lowered their masks. She had a partial view of their faces. Paisley had a thick mustache. Gray's hard, square jawline was covered in heavy stubble.

"Put it on speaker when you answer it," Paisley said, while Becca strained to hear them.

Gray gave the other man a slight nod as he reached for the receiver. He picked up the phone and hit a button. "Hello. Who is this?"

"This is Special Agent Jake Delgado with the FBI," a deep voice said on the other end through the speaker, and Becca's heart stalled a beat.

Emotion sprang up in her that was immediate and visceral. All of it tied to the intimacy they'd shared, every kiss, every caress, every smile—every argument—and to this moment, when she needed him to bring to bear the attributes that had earned him the nickname "the miracle worker."

She might not be able to trust him with her heart, but she prayed she could trust him with her life since it was now in his hands.

"FBI?" Gray asked. "What are you doing here? There are no field offices in Wyoming. The closest one is two hours away. Is this big enough for you to fly in?"

"Looks like someone has done his homework. Who am I speaking with?"

Looking at the other guy, Gray hesitated. "You can call me Mister," he said.

"I gave you my name. I would prefer to know yours."

Not only was Jake trying to learn the man's identity, but calling someone by their name built familiarity. It was a stepping-stone to establishing a bond.

"I bet you would," Gray responded, "but I don't care about your preferences. You don't need my name. All you need to know is that I'm the man in charge."

"It's good to speak with you, Mister," Jake said. "It sounds as if you have a plan. How does all this play out?"

"With us winning. Finally. For once in our lives."

"What do you hope to win?"

"Guess you'll have to wait and see," Gray said, and Jake paused, a long time. So long that Gray asked, "Are you still there?"

"I'm here. Listening. Wondering. Is everyone in there okay?"

"We haven't hurt anyone. They're all fine," Gray said. "If you want them to stay fit as a fiddle, then you need to keep your people back and away from the doors."

"We only have a visual on four of the hostages. You

have four more adults that we're aware of and six minors," Jake said. "Is our count of the number of hostages you're holding accurate?"

"Yeah. You've got it right."

"Can you put one of them on the phone?" Jake asked. "To verify the others are all right?"

The two gunmen looked to each other. Gray seemed uncertain about how to answer, but he said, "No. The others are indisposed. They can't come to the phone."

"Where are you holding them?"

"In a room."

"I hope it's close to a bathroom. Eventually they'll need to go. You don't want to have to haul folks all the way downstairs to use the facilities."

"Nobody is upstairs," Gray said. "The story time room is close enough to the restroom."

"That's good. The less stress for you right now the better," Jake said. "I'm sure you don't want to be in this situation. You've obviously reached some kind of crisis point in your life and feel you have no other option. I'd like to understand your position better so that I can help you get this resolved. Why don't you tell me what you want?"

"I want national news coverage for starters. So far this is only being reported on the local news."

"Why is it so important that you have national coverage?" Jake asked.

"Because I want the whole world to see what we're doing here. I want as many people as possible to know."

To see how they invaded a public library and took

people captive? Or to witness them doing something far worse? To her and the kids?

Jake wouldn't have to lift a finger to meet their first demand. It was only a matter of time before this story became breaking news across the top media outlets.

But then what would happen to all of them being held prisoner once the nation was watching?

Dreadful thoughts spun in her mind.

"What do you want everyone to know?" Jake asked. "Why don't you share it with me now? Believe it or not, I'm here to help you get what you want."

"Then get this on every major news network. Once you do that, we'll talk." Gray slammed down the receiver, ending the call. He turned away from the phone, giving Becca a full-frontal view of his face.

If she could snap a picture of him and send it to Jake, it would help him identify at least one assailant faster. She reached for her boot to pull out the cell phone that she had hidden. As she slipped her hand inside and grasped the edge of the phone, Gray's gaze lifted in her direction.

Their eyes met across the distance.

Swearing, she ducked down on pure instinct. But it was already too late.

He'd seen her.

"ANY INSIGHT INTO our unsub?" Nash asked. "Think he's done this kind of thing before?"

"He's thought this through. That's for sure," Jake said. "Prepped and planned, obviously. But I got the impression that this is his first time." It was in the way he responded to certain questions. The hesitation.

Jake often used deliberate pauses strategically. On Mister's end of the conversation, it had felt like uncertainty.

"Is that it?" Guidry asked, his tone scathing. "I had heard you were the best, but you didn't make any progress. What in the hell was that?"

Straightening, Jake was determined to maintain his composure despite his frustration over how the initial contact had gone. He had nothing to work with. "I'd call it a good start."

"You don't have proof of life on the rest of the hostages," Guidry said, raising a finger. "No assurance the kids aren't hurt. You don't have the name of a single kidnapper. And you don't know what they want. I wouldn't call that *good*."

Staring at Guidry's four raised fingers, Jake gritted his teeth. "At a minimum this got the ball rolling with open communication."

"More than that," Nash said, jumping in. "Jake got him to confirm the total number of hostages. We now know where in the library they're being held, in the event we need to breach the building. All vital information. He did good."

They had been able to identify the four male hostages that were strapped to chairs inside the library near the doors. Sheriff Clark hadn't released any names to the media yet. They were going to keep those quiet for a while longer, especially those of the minors and Becca since she was a federal agent. The media had been pushed too far back to get a look at the hostages that had been positioned near the second set of double doors.

Although Jake would have liked a glimpse of Becca, to see that she was all right, at least she was in a room with Mason, away from the entrances and windows in case something happened.

"Once this story hits the national news, meeting their first demand," Jake said, "I can push them harder to give me something in return."

But it troubled him that they had insisted on major coverage before talking to him further. Maybe they were waiting for the world to tune in only to detonate a bomb. Or to start a killing spree. Maybe they had no intention of speaking to him again and wanted to make a statement with carnage.

They obviously wanted attention, but to what end?

"This will go national with or without any action by you," Guidry said.

"It will. But they still asked, and once it happens, they'll think I delivered. Perception is all that matters." To the kidnappers, Jake would have acted in good faith—an essential step in the process—giving them something they wanted, establishing a building block of trust.

"Still didn't do much to move things forward, is my point," Guidry said. "The mayor expects progress."

Jake drew in a deep breath. "Every parent out there not only expects it, but they deserve it, and they'll get it. But on my terms. Not yours."

"You'll make it happen." Nash put a hand on his

shoulder. "You've done it a hundred times before, Jake. You'll do it again."

Jake nodded even as the frustration he was hiding swelled. A part of him agreed with Guidry, that little voice inside his head that constantly told him he wasn't doing enough.

His future brother-in-law looked at Guidry. "Do you have any actual advice? Or just unhelpful criticism?"

"Merely sharing my observations." Guidry took a seat and crossed his legs. "It would be nice if you could work a little faster so those kids being held at gunpoint in there could sleep in their own beds tonight."

Yes, it would.

"Instead of working faster, I choose to work smarter. Passing time releases tension, giving things a chance to deescalate," Jake said, raising a finger. "It allows us the opportunity to gather intelligence. With some much-needed blanks filled in, we can improve the plan." And it would refine how he would approach things when they next spoke. "Sometimes these things end simply by waiting them out because they don't want to go any longer without food and being exhausted. Mental fatigue weakens motivational willpower. Then they've also got the hassle of tending to the hostages, which will wear on them. Gaining their trust is a matter of give-and-take that doesn't happen with the snap of a finger. It's a process. Negotiations are temporal. Whoever dominates time is in charge. So, the longer they're in there, thinking they're in full control, the better."

Holding up his hands, with seven fingers raised, Jake was grateful that Guidry had finally shut up.

This situation boiled down to influence through communication. Although Jake had successfully made contact, he'd failed to get them to reveal anything about themselves or their motives. Essentially, he was operating blind, but even in the dark he knew the way forward.

After Jake got Mister talking, he needed to make them feel like he understood their side of the matter. Then he could begin building tactical empathy by exploring the feelings underlying their demands. All his efforts were to get them to trust him. Once that happened, he could work on the problem with them. Suggest a course of action that would keep everyone breathing.

If everything went according to plan, the assailants would demonstrate a behavioral change. The release of a hostage. Perhaps even surrender.

"I'll go update the mayor. It'll keep him from barging in and disrupting things." Guidry stood. "Since we're going to be here a while, I'll make arrangements for food, but it will be billed to the FBI." With that, he trudged out of the tent.

"That's probably as close to an apology as you'll get without him losing face," Nash said.

"I don't need an apology. I just need him to stay out of my way." Jake whipped out his cell and dialed his field office. Special Agent Tracy Morris answered. "Hey, Tracy. What's the ETA on the mobile command center?"

"It should be there in less than forty minutes," she said. "Aaron is bringing it up."

Special Agent Aaron Vance. He was a tech guru that

Jake had worked with many times, and he was easy to get along with.

"Okay, great. Is he alone or is Debbie with him?"

Dr. Deborah Holmes was a clinical psychologist who usually accompanied his negotiation team. She often gave them invaluable insight.

Psychologists generally weren't effective as negotiators because hostage takers resented the implication that they were mentally ill. Debbie acted as a consultant. Her most important role was to monitor the behavior of the team members, particularly Jake's position as primary negotiator, and assess their reactions to the stressful situation. She could offer emotional support to the team, possibly alert the team leader—in this case Nash, who was sticking his neck out—if there was any undesirable impact of stress on the negotiator's behavior and provide post-trauma counseling for the hostages.

"Debbie is a no-go," Tracy said. "She's on vacation. We tried contacting her, but she's camping in the Rocky Mountain National Park and her cell service is dodgy."

They were going to need a replacement. Preferably one who knew him well. In all the cases he had been on, he needed a psychologist on this one the most. Not only to catch any red flags in his behavior, which would help protect Nash, but to also counsel the hostages afterward, especially the teenagers.

"Can you do me a favor?" he asked. "At least get started on it until Aaron arrives and can take over?"

"Sure," Tracy said. "What do you want me to do?"

"I need everything you can dig up on Leonard

Guidry, a private contractor, who is currently head of security for Mayor Schroeder."

"Can do. I'll get on it and send Aaron whatever I find."

Disconnecting the call, he turned to Nash. "We need a replacement for Dr. Debbie Holmes." He quickly explained the many reasons why. "Do you think Lynn could fill in for her?" As a qualified, licensed psychotherapist with a PhD, Lynn used to treat people with severe pathologies and now ran an anger management and domestic violence program.

"I can't think of anyone better to let me know if you're about to go off the deep end," Nash said. "And she's only twenty minutes away. I'll call her."

BECCA SCURRIED BACK across the room to where she had been seated. Bracing herself for what might happen next, she drew in a slow, steady breath as she watched Gray and Paisley approaching the room through the window.

Both had covered their mouths and noses again, but anger simmered in their eyes.

"Go get her!" Gray said, standing in front of the room.

Paisley pulled out the keys, unlocked the door, and threw it open, making it slam against the wall. He stalked inside toward her.

Mason curled a hand around her arm. "Aunt Becca?"

"Don't worry," she whispered. "Stay seated."

Paisley prowled up to her and snatched her by the hair. "Get up," he said, yanking her to her feet.

Startling pain seared through her scalp. Swallowing a gasp, she grabbed the hand locked onto her hair, keeping him from tugging her head, and punched the inside of his arm a couple of inches up from the elbow, hitting the sweet spot.

On reflex, he released her hair and dropped his arm.

The move had been pure instinct on her part. She had acted without thinking but had managed to stop herself before she kneed him in the groin and punched his throat.

"You bitch!" Paisley slapped her hard, the force of it stinging her cheek. "I'll teach you." He smacked the other side of her face with the back of his hand, drawing a shriek from one of the girls, and making both her cheeks burn.

Her eyes watered as a knot of fury tightened in her throat. Becca had to swallow hard against it. She was capable of taking this man on and disarming him, but not before the other one—who was also armed and standing a few feet away—interceded. He could shoot her, threaten the kids, possibly even her nephew. She had no choice but to stand there and take it.

Paisley drew back to hit her again.

"Craig!" Gray yelled at him. "That's enough. What's wrong with you? She's pregnant."

"I didn't hit her in the belly. Only in her pretty face. She'll be fine."

Gray swore at him. "Just get her out of the room."

There was a sharp sting near the corner of her mouth. Becca licked her lips and tasted blood. Her face was on fire, but through the humiliating burn was the sweet balm of success. She had gotten a first name, which was more than she'd had earlier.

The man she now knew as Craig drew his Glock and pointed it at her head. "Walk."

Doing like she was told, she glanced over her shoulder at Mason to reassure him that she was all right.

"Don't look back at them." Craig nudged her shoulder with the barrel, urging her forward. "Go on."

She stepped out of the room, coming face-to-face with Gray, but what she saw in his eyes gave her pause. He looked weary, not angry. "Restrain her."

Craig pulled out a zip tie from his pocket. He bound her wrists together in front of her, tightening the restraint until the plastic cut into her flesh, making her wince. He locked the story time room.

Then Gray snatched her arm, leading her two doors down to a small study room. It had a table, four chairs and a glass window like the story time room. "Get rid of the chairs," he said to Craig, "and check in with the others."

While Craig followed the order, she noticed he wasn't wearing gloves anymore. As he passed her, she caught sight of a tattoo on his hand, on the area of skin between the thumb and the index finger. A black spider.

After the chairs were removed, Craig tossed Gray the keys and left to carry out the other orders.

Gray shoved her inside. "Maybe a little alone time will help clear your head so you can make better choices. Don't do anything that stupid again. Otherwise, I don't know if I can protect you."

This was the opening she'd been waiting for. Gray

wasn't exactly what he appeared to be if he was concerned about her welfare. "A heartless monster wouldn't care less about protecting me. But that doesn't seem like you."

"Because it's not. None of us are."

Oh, really. "Then why are you acting like monsters, taking hostages at gunpoint? Children? Slapping me around?"

"I'm sorry about Craig," Gray said, with a shake of his head as if hating what had happened. "He's always lacked the proper respect for women. He's incurable. Not even therapy could help that man, but I needed him for this. I know how all this must look now, but, honestly, we're trying to be heroes."

Becca narrowed her eyes at that. "Whatever you're hoping to achieve, this isn't the right way," she said, wanting him to see reason. "Heroes don't endanger the lives of others."

"We haven't hurt anybody. We hope we don't have to," Gray said, sounding sincere.

"Why are you doing this?" she asked.

"Because it's the only way. When you're taking on a powerful enemy, extreme measures are necessary." He sighed. "Will you cooperate by keeping your head down and being quiet, instead of snooping? Can I count on you not to be a problem?"

Most definitely not. "Yes. Head down and keep quiet."

"Once you prove it, I'll let you rejoin the others. Mess up again and next time the consequences will be more severe. I'd rather not strap a woman, especially a pregnant one, to a chair in front of the doors of the entrances. No bathroom. No food. No water. For however long this takes."

"You brought food with you?" There were no vending machines in the library, so they must have.

"Sure did. Figured we might be here a while."

They were prepared for this to be drawn out. Jake was probably counting on them not having any food. Negotiators often relied on hunger and fatigue on the part of the captors to help resolve things.

"But if you push me, you won't get a single crumb or drop of water," Gray said. "Whatever happens to your baby after that will be on you. Got it?"

Stiffening at the warning, Becca believed that he would follow through. She nodded, torn at what to do. If she risked doing her job, trying to help Jake save the hostages, she might jeopardize the well-being of her unborn child. But if she did nothing and someone got hurt or died because she'd chosen to put herself first, could she live with it?

Choices determined who you were and this one required sacrifice.

Chapter Five

Brian hustled alongside Rocco, headed for the blue-and-white FBI mobile command center that had arrived.

All the civilians had been moved away from the scene. An armored vehicle had been placed near each entrance of the library, to be used as cover if necessary. A helicopter from the sheriff's department hovered overhead along with two others from local news stations.

Total darkness had fallen. The sweltering heat from earlier had dropped to a temperate degree. Floodlights had been set up around the library, illuminating it bright as a football stadium.

The White House press secretary, followed by a representative from the Pentagon, had wrapped up their briefings along with question-and-answer sessions. The hostage incident at the public library in Laramie had been breaking news for a bit across every major network.

Brian was aware that Jake was only waiting to find out what he and Rocco had learned before calling the hostage takers again. Brian climbed the steps to the side door of the truck and tried the handle. Finding it locked, he rapped his knuckles on the door. "It's Bradshaw and Sharp," he said.

Jake wanted to minimize the number of personnel in the command center.

One of the cameras mounted on the vehicle swiveled and lowered toward them before the door swung open. Nash let them in.

Entering first, Brian looked around. The space was dimly lit, allowing the wall at the far back with four different screens showing various angles of the library and surrounding area to be the focus. A red digital clock above the screens served as a reminder of how pressing this was. He'd never been in one of the FBI's mobile units before. The trailer was equipped with top-of-the-line technology, all the communication and surveillance equipment, and workspaces for at least four. He was impressed.

Leo Guidry sat in a chair far from Jake. Brian's gaze met Guidry's, but the man didn't acknowledge him.

The back door closed, and the lock snapped into place.

"Brian Bradshaw, Rocco Sharp," Jake said, glancing between them, "this is Dr. Lynn Delgado." He gestured to the attractive woman at his side. "She's joining the team as a psychological consultant."

"Your sister and your fiancée," Brian said, gesturing to Jake and Nash. "We've seen you in Delgado's, but finally, we get a proper introduction." The entire team had heard about Lynn's extraordinary ordeal last winter and how Nash had gone above and beyond to rescue her. But Nash had never brought her, the so-called love of his life, by the office or out for drinks with the team. The man liked to keep his personal life separate from the professional side.

"It's nice to meet you both as well," Lynn said, shaking their hands. "Nash never talks about his team."

"No surprise there," Rocco said. "I'm only shocked that he was able to talk enough to get engaged at all, much less to a shrink."

It must've been like pulling teeth for Lynn to get Nash to open up. To call the man brusque would be a gross understatement. If she got him to pour out his heart and share his deepest thoughts—which would be short of a miracle—then she was probably fantastic at her job.

"All right." Frowning, Nash shook his head. "That's enough. We've got work to do."

"Tell me one or both of you have got something," Jake said.

Brian decided to take the lead on debriefing. "Traffic cameras caught the two white vans on the way to the library," he said. "Unfortunately, we can't pinpoint exactly where they came from. Only that it was somewhere from the north side of town. An image of the driver of the lead van was captured, but his face was only partially visible. There is a storefront security camera that might have a better angle, but the proprietor is refusing to grant us access. We can get a warrant, but it'll take a little time. I mentioned it to the sheriff on my way in and he'll do his best to get it fast-tracked. I wish I had better news."

"Who would refuse to cooperate during an active crime with hostages involved, some of them children?"

Nash asked, voicing the same question that had been lingering in Brian's head.

"Send over what you've got on the image of the driver. Aaron," Jake said, and their tech guru seated in front of a computer raised his hand, "might be able to work with the partial."

Brian had anticipated that. "Done. I already sent the file over."

Jake turned to Aaron.

"On it," Aaron replied without Jake needing to utter a word. The sharp clacking of computer keys followed.

"And I'll see to it that Daniel doesn't have any hiccups with the warrant," Nash added.

Though he doubted the sheriff would run into any issues, Brian nodded. In the event Sheriff Clark did, the FBI had the power to make it happen quickly. "The two white vans were reported stolen first thing this morning by a local charity after they opened and discovered the vehicles were missing."

"Do you think they were taken sometime overnight?" Jake asked.

"I'm assuming." Which Brian hated to do. It led to mistakes. He glanced at the digital clock on the back wall. It was almost eleven at night. "In the morning, my next step is to swing by there, confirm that, and see whether they caught anything on their security cameras. I was also thinking I should speak with the owners of the vehicles who had their license plates pilfered," Brian said. "Maybe the kidnappers were neighbors and decided to boost convenient plates. Or perhaps the plates were taken in a parking lot of a store, where there might be extra security footage. On the police report, neither owner could say with certainty when the plates were taken. Only when they realized they were missing."

People had a tendency to dismiss details that they had considered minor. Helping them backtrack might lead to something.

"Sounds like a plan." Jake looked at Rocco. "Did we get anything from forensics?"

The ATF agent looked rough and tough—make no mistake, he was—but Brian had seen a softer side to him as well around animals and kids. Rocco even assisted his cousin, Charlie, at the Underground Self-Defense School, teaching women essential life-saving skills. Brian had volunteered to help, if they could use him. But Charlie had refused to even shake his hand and flat-out rejected his offer with no explanation. You would've thought Brian had leprosy. Charlie Sharp was as aloof as she was alluring, and he was dying to get to know her better.

The one thing going for him was that he was not only coworkers with her cousin, but good friends, too.

Rocco frowned at Jake's question, and Brian knew that no one was going to like what he had to say. "Forensics turned up nothing. The van had been wiped clean. Even the gas tank cap. They thought this through. There was one weird thing. The vans hadn't been hotwired. The keys were sitting in the ignition."

"Maybe they managed to get their hands on the keys when they pinched the vehicles from the charity," Nash said.

"Possible." Brian gave a nod. "I'll find out when I go by there tomorrow."

Rocco ran a hand across the scruff on his jaw. "I had an idea. Since they fired off their weapons outside, there are quite a few shell casings."

Jake must've seen where Rocco was going with this. "Isn't it difficult to lift prints off of bullet casings?"

"Yeah, it is." Rocco nodded. "The casings are exposed to gunpowder residue, hot temperatures and high pressure. Fingerprint compounds such as amino acids and lipids often evaporate or degrade by the time they're ejected from a weapon. Getting a usable print from whatever is lift is challenging. But not impossible."

"Okay," Jake said. "We'll send someone out to collect them. The process could be tricky. If the person was spotted getting too close to the building, it could antagonize the kidnappers."

Rocco flashed a grim smile. "The casings have already been collected. I took care of it. Got them bagged and handed over to forensics."

Brian had witnessed Rocco in action, slithering like a snake on his belly, wearing gloves, collecting casings around the Grand Avenue entrance. His buddy had reminded Brian of his military days. The *low crawl* was a movement used by the army to create the lowest silhouette while crossing places where the concealment was sparse and enemy fire was possible.

"You could've gotten your head blown off," Nash said.

A point that Brian had also made. There was no talking the guy out of it. Rocco was the one on the team who would drop anything if you were in trouble and do anything to help get you out of it. Becca needed them all right now.

"But I didn't," Rocco countered, popping a piece of gum in his mouth. "My head is still intact."

Rocco always showed steely confidence, but Brian realized the low-crawling mission had stressed him a bit. The only kind of gum he chewed was medicated with nicotine, which meant that his friend was having a craving.

Jake folded his arms. "While I appreciate your initiative, your actions could have endangered the hostages. Going forward, it's better to ask permission than beg forgiveness. Not the other way around. Are we clear?"

"Crystal," Rocco said, chewing his gum. "But if we get a print, I'd like a *thank-you*."

"Fair enough. I've got no problem showing appreciation when it's due. Let's see if we get anything first."

Rocco gave a curt nod. "You got it."

"The hostage takers should have seen plenty of the news coverage by now," Jake said. "I'm going to reach out to them. If you don't need to be in here, this is a good time to clear out."

Brian wanted nothing more than to hear firsthand what kind of progress Jake would be able to make. Unfortunately, he wouldn't be able to stick around. But Becca needed the best negotiator on this. Supposedly that was Agent Delgado.

They would all see if he would live up to his reputation. For Becca's sake, he had better.

TAKING A SEAT by the command center phone, Jake got ready while Brian and Rocco left the command center.

Unfortunately, Guidry hung back. At least he wasn't talking.

Once the mobile command center was on-site along with SWAT—snipers in position on the rooftops of nearby buildings and in a couple of trees and an explosives expert standing by—Jake had found his footing while Guidry had found a seat on the sidelines, observing quietly. As he should be.

It also didn't hurt having his sister on the team, watching his and Nash's backs. They had gotten Lynn up to speed on relevant details that hadn't been released to the media. He'd shared his opinion that he didn't think the lead unsub was mentally disturbed, but Lynn would listen in on future calls and give her assessment.

The standoff had been going on for over six hours. Despite not having more intel to go on, Jake dialed the private number to the library and waited as the line rang.

Lynn was seated to his right. Nash stood on his left.

"Hello," a gruff male voice said over speaker. It sounded like Mister.

"This is Jake." Deliberately he'd dropped his title and surname. He wanted the kidnapper to feel like it wasn't necessary. This was about two human beings communicating, understanding one another. "The story is on every major network like you wanted."

"I'm aware." Mister hesitated.

Jake sensed something was wrong. "You got what you wanted. You should be pleased."

"It's just that I want to speak to them. To the reporters. Explain our side of things."

Asking for airtime where they spoke to the press, was unusual. "Explain it to me," Jake said, softening his voice. "I'm here and I'm listening."

"No way!" Mister's tone grew irritated. "So you can silence me? First, the world hears what I have to say. I want you to send in some reporters. Not just anyone. I want to talk to a couple of big-time journalists who will get what I have to say out on more than one major network. Understand?"

Tensing, Jake didn't immediately respond. "I'm sorry, but I can't do that," he said. "I can't give you more civilians to hold captive."

"What? I have no intention of keeping them. I'll let them go after I say my piece."

"I'm sorry," Jake repeated. "That's not going to happen. But I have another way for you to share your story."

"How?" Mister asked, sounding skeptical.

"We send you a bullhorn. You address them through a window."

A grim laugh rolled over the phone line. "Where you shoot me?"

"I'd like it if no one got shot," Jake said, honestly. The first priority in a hostage situation was the preservation of life, but if he had to give the SWAT leader the go-ahead to take someone out, he would. "Open a window of your choice. We'll toss in a bullhorn. You stay low, where you're concealed, and address the press. I'll pull back the choppers and they'll be able to hear you. That's the best I can do."

More hesitation from Mister. "Okay. We'll break a window on the west side of the building on Seventh,"

Mister said, referring to the street where the command center was parked. "You deliver the bullhorn personally, Agent Delgado."

"Call me Jake," he said, and his sister nodded in encouragement. "I will be the one to bring it, but I'm going to need you to give me something first. As a show of good faith."

"Like what?"

"Release some of the hostages," Jake said.

"Nope. I'm not doing it."

"You want something big. A chance to address the world. I need something big in return." Jake paused a beat. "At least let the kids go. Otherwise, no bullhorn."

Guidry stood and strode closer.

"How do I know that if we get close to the doors that those snipers won't open fire?" Mister asked.

The question was a good sign. It meant he was seriously considering releasing the teens.

"You have my word," he said.

"Your word doesn't mean squat, Jake."

More progress. He had used his first name. "You designate the entrance," Jake said. "I'll be there to escort the kids away from the building. The snipers take orders from me. No one is cleared to fire because taking one of you out doesn't solve my problem. It will only make the situation worse for the hostages. What do you say?"

"Will you be unarmed?" Mister asked.

Hope rose inside Jake. "Yes."

"I'll give you four of the six kids."

Nash shook his head and hit the mute button. "Why wouldn't he simply give us all of them?"

"Which four?" Guidry asked, reminding them of his one and only priority. The mayor's son.

Raising her palms for their questions to stop, Lynn said, "Give him space to work. He's been through this many times. He knows what he's doing."

Giving his sister a nod of thanks, Jake unmuted the call. His mind snapped into sharper focus. "I need all the kids."

"Big difference between necessity and desire. You *want* all six. I'm offering four. That's the best I'll do."

To Jake, it didn't matter which four, but he saw an opportunity here that could prove fruitful down the road. "Who would you be keeping hostage?"

"The Schroeder boy and the Pietsch girl."

With his jaw clenched, Nash shook his head again.

Guidry cursed under his breath. "That's unacceptable," he whispered. "You can't let that happen."

The captors knew precisely who they had and the value of those two particular hostages.

"Paige and Tyler?" Jake asked. The more often their names were used, the more human they became instead of simply being bargaining chips. It was a technique that had the power to save lives. "Why do you want to keep Paige and Tyler?"

"I think you know why."

Jake exchanged a glance with Nash as Guidry folded his arms across his chest. Aaron was paying attention while still focusing on his tasks. Lynn looked at him expectantly, support radiating from her.

"I need *all six* kids," Jake said.

"Some is better than none. Right?" Mister added.

Another tactic Jake had employed in the past was to say nothing after a captor had given him an offer. The silence implied that the deal wasn't good enough and there was the fact that people instinctively didn't like the awkwardness of it. They felt the need to fill in the space by upping the ante.

In many hostage negotiations it had worked. It had also gotten him 5 percent extra the last time he had sold a house. Silence truly was golden.

"I won't give up Paige and Tyler, hear me," Mister finally said, using their names, which was a tiny win that Jake took, "but I'm willing to give you somebody else instead. A pregnant woman."

Becca.

It had to be.

The captors had placed four men in front of the doors of the library. There were only four adult hostages left. Two were women and Abigail Abshire was long past her childbearing years.

Flicking a glance at Nash, he saw on his face that he had also done the math and realized how deeply personal this really was for Jake.

Slowly, Lynn was piecing it together, her eyes narrowing with concern.

"Okay," Jake said. "But I'll need proof of life on Paige and Tyler. As well as the other hostages we haven't been able to see. Abigail Abshire, Cameron Lund and Russell Nolan."

"You'll get proof when I release the kids through the window."

"Why not through the front or rear doors?" Jake wondered.

"We're not going to give you the chance to pull something," Mister said. "Be out there in five minutes. Kill the floodlights on that side of the building. I don't want to see anybody else but you, and tell those snipers to hold their fire while we open the window." Mister hung up.

Guidry swore out loud. "What were you thinking? How could you let them keep the mayor's son?" he asked.

Jake looked at his watch, keeping track of the deadline rather than feeding into Guidry's hysterics. "I was thinking about the five lives I can save in the next four and a half minutes."

Getting Becca out meant everything to him, but he had been willing to settle for just the four teens. Mister had made a legitimate point.

Some were better than none.

Jake would work on getting all the others out of this unharmed.

"Unbelievable! You had the chance to play hardball and get Tyler out of there and you squandered it. Those animals would've accepted any deal you insisted on in order to get their fifteen minutes of fame."

His sister stood. "Mr. Guidry, I think you need to take a breath and lower your voice."

"I'm fine," he snapped.

"Your anger and hostility are not fine," Lynn said. "This emotional outburst is counterproductive. I suggest you get some air."

Glaring at her, Guidry stormed out of the command center and slammed the door behind him.

"We're going to hear about this from the mayor," Nash said. "And it's going to be ugly."

Nodding, Jake understood it was about to hit the fan.

"Is what he said about Becca true?" Nash asked. "Is she pregnant?"

Aaron swiveled in his chair and stared at Jake, along with Lynn, who was also waiting to hear the answer.

Saying it out loud would make it real. Jake couldn't handle that now. There wasn't time to spare. He picked up the radio and contacted the SWAT team leader. "This is Agent Delgado."

"Utley here."

"The HTs," he said, using the abbreviation for hostage takers, "are going to open a window on the west side of the building that faces Seventh Street. Kill the floodlights on that side of the building and hold your fire. They are planning to release five hostages in exchange for a bullhorn so they can make a statement to the media. I repeat, no one is to take a shot. Do you get it?"

"I read you loud and clear. If anything changes, let me know," Utley said. "My guys are ready."

"Thanks." Jake disconnected. He took off his lightweight sport jacket and then removed his gun from the holster and handed his sidearm to Nash.

"Jake?" Lynn asked, meeting his eyes.

But he couldn't hold her penetrating gaze. "I can't. Not now." He grabbed a jacket with FBI stenciled on the back and slipped it on over his T-shirt. "Hey, Aaron, I hope you and Tracy have dug up something on Guidry because I could use it right about now."

With a grim expression, Aaron said, "Guidry's record is quite impressive." Then he grinned. "Because half of it is fluff. He was once a third-rate negotiator for a private hostage rescue firm. On his last case with that company in San Bernadino, he snapped and lost his temper during a twenty-seven-hour standoff, screaming at one of the captors who had a gun to a hostage's head. He was lucky the victim wasn't killed. After he was fired, Guidry went to work for his father-in-law's security company. They padded his résumé and shipped him off to Wyoming, where they thought he couldn't get himself into any more trouble."

Banging on the side door drew their attention.

"It's them," Aaron said, glancing at the screen for the security camera. "The mayor, the councilwoman and your favorite contractor."

"Perfect timing with the info on Guidry," Jake said to their tech guru. "Thanks."

Aaron gave a two-finger salute. "You got it."

The banging intensified, echoing throughout the trailer.

"Ready for this?" Nash asked.

Would he ever be? "Let's get it over with," Jake said.

Nash unlocked and opened the door.

Chapter Six

Gray, or Mister, as he wanted to be called over the phone, had not made an idle threat. And Becca wasn't taking it lightly.

She understood the danger and the consequences. Being moved from the safety of a room to the front line. Being restrained, unable to protect herself. Denied food and water when she needed both frequently in her condition.

But she was still the same person. An FBI agent sworn to uphold the law. A fighter who would never cower to bullies or tyrants or criminals. She would never back down from doing the right thing.

If she was able to get any information that could help Jake get everyone through this safely, then she was obligated to do so.

Rising on her knees, she peered through the window.

Gray had finished his call at the information desk, presumably with Jake, and was now speaking with Blue. From the study room, which was farther away from the information desk, she couldn't overhear what they were saying from this distance. Also, with the more limited vantage point, she couldn't see Craig, either. Maybe he had switched positions with the other man and was keeping watch near one of the entrances.

The good news was that Gray and Blue had both lowered their masks. The two men spoke freely and at ease with each other as though they were close friends. They seemed engrossed in their conversation.

Another opportunity such as this to photograph the faces of two of their captors might not come along. Learning their identities was crucial to Jake if he had any hope of ending this situation sooner rather than later.

She had to take the risk.

Ducking back down, she shoved her bound hands into her boot. The fit was tight. Her fingers gripped the top of the cell and she managed to slide it out. Her palm tingled holding it—a lifeline to the outside world. To Jake. The phone was the only tool she had to help him and thereby herself and the others.

Becca entered the simplistic passcode that was basically worthless. The phone only had 30 percent power left. She accessed the camera function, making sure the flash and sound connected to the app were turned off.

She crawled to the corner of the room. Slowly, she eased up only enough to peer out the window.

They were still talking. Gray looked at his watch, checking the time.

She lifted the camera and began snapping photos of both men. They kept shifting their stances, pacing as they spoke, enabling her to capture images of their full faces.

Now all she had to do was send them to Jake. Her need to reach him, send the pictures and hear his voice was nearly overwhelming, but so was her concern over getting caught.

Her gaze swung once again to the gunmen. Neither was looking in her direction. She glanced back at the phone, with her heart in her throat, her fingers itching to tap the call icon.

Then Blue hollered for Craig, stopping her. Seconds later, the short, stocky guy appeared. They swapped places, with Blue grabbing a small bottle of water from the duffel bag before going toward the rear entrance.

Gray called out to him, "Refill that from the fountain. If they shut off the water, we'll need the rest."

"Yeah, all right."

Pulling up their masks, Gray and Craig turned toward the story room and headed that way with their guns drawn.

Becca ducked down.

Something must have been happening.

Had Jake negotiated the release of a hostage? Or were they about to make an example out of one of them, showing the authorities that they were willing to hurt people to get what they wanted?

Either way, they might come to check on her.

Quickly, she powered off the phone and stuffed it deep down in her boot. No sooner had she sat down with her back to the wall than the door to the study room swung open.

Her heart pounded at how close she had come to being caught for a second time. If she had been, it would've been for nothing, since she hadn't had time to send Jake the pictures.

"Get up," Gray said.

She did as she was told.

He drew a knife and cut her zip tie. "You're coming with me."

A RED-FACED WILLIAM SCHROEDER and overwrought Felicia Pietsch barged inside the mobile command center, with Guidry bringing up the rear.

"You need to get all the kids out of there," the mayor said, wagging a finger, fury emanating from him, "or heads will roll. I can get the governor on the phone any time, day or night. We will have someone's badge if you fail to get our children out of that library."

"The goal is to get everyone out." Jake clipped his badge onto his belt, where it would be prominently displayed. "We'll get four kids and a pregnant woman now. The rest later."

"Later when?" the mayor demanded, anger stamped all over his face.

Ignoring the mounting pressure in the space and the fact that everyone was staring at him, Jake made a noncommittal gesture. "I don't know for certain." He didn't have a crystal ball, though he wishcd like hell that he did.

"I told you he couldn't hack it," Guidry said, the vitriol practically seeping out of his pores. "He's just going to leave your kids in there for only God knows how long. I hope they walk out of there and don't have to be carried out in body bags after he blows it."

Pietsch gasped and swayed on her feet.

Lynn gripped the councilwoman's arm, steadying

her. "That's out of line, Mr. Guidry. You don't need to stoke the flames, feeding these parents' worst fears."

"It's *my hope*," Jake said, staring at the contractor, "that this will be resolved in under twenty-seven hours." He picked the time frame from Guidry's botched assignment, to catch his attention. "Less time than the standoff you were involved in out in San Bernardino."

All the blood drained from Guidry's face as his eyes didn't just widen, they almost bugged out of his head. His mouth closed, his lips thinning into a line.

"Oh, God," Pietsch said. "Twenty-seven hours. No, no, that's too long. Paige can't stay in there overnight. She'll die."

It might take even longer than that, but these terrified parents didn't want to hear a speech from him about how time was their friend and not the enemy.

Where was the sheriff when he needed him? Daniel Clark should be keeping them calm and out of the way.

"Take deep steady breaths," Lynn said, guiding Pietsch to sit in a chair.

"We have the situation under control," Jake said, trying to reassure the councilwoman. "The negotiation has just begun. I believe we can resolve this without any of the hostages dying."

Mister was open to cooperation and had already agreed to release some of the hostages. This was a great sign that it could end peacefully.

"No, you don't understand," Pietsch said. "Paige has type 1 diabetes. If she doesn't get an insulin shot tonight…" The stricken mother broke down in tears. "My daughter could die. Please. The stress of this, even if she had her shot, could send her into shock," she said, sobbing. "She hasn't eaten. Her blood sugar levels haven't been tested. I tell her all the time to carry snacks with her because she can only have certain things. High in protein. Low in carbohydrates. Low in sugar. But she doesn't listen. Teenagers think they're invincible. She could go into a coma. Or die. Please, you have to get her out of there. Now." Mrs. Pietsch cried harder, sagging against the computer console.

This was a complication that could lead to dire consequences. A teenage girl's life was at stake. Why hadn't Pietsch shared this essential information sooner? He could've factored it into his strategy before he had negotiated and agreed to Mister's terms.

How was he going to convince the captors to give up the councilwoman's daughter now?

Jake looked at his watch. Forty-five seconds. "I have to get out there. They're expecting to see me. I can't miss this deadline."

Pietsch jumped to her feet and clutched his arm, desperation welling in her light brown eyes. "What about Paige?" Tears streamed down her face, making her mascara run. "What are you going to do? You can't let her die in there."

Jake struggled to stay above water with this emotional tide threatening to drown him. "I'll do what I can for her." He patted her hand and moved out of her grasp. "And for all the other hostages." He grabbed the bullhorn, pushed past the parents and Guidry, and stepped outside.

Hot on his heels was Nash, coming up beside him. "I need an answer. Is Becca pregnant?"

Jake's chest tightened. "Yes."

"Is it yours?" Nash asked, marching around the trailer with him.

"Yes."

Clenching his jaw, Nash grunted. "You neglected to mention that. I assumed things were casual between you guys."

Me, too.

"Why didn't you tell me you two were serious?" Nash asked.

"I've got a job to do and fifteen seconds to be in front of that window. This conversation has to wait."

"You've got to get this right," Nash said, holding his gaze. "Do whatever it takes to get that girl out of there."

That went without saying. Jake wasn't going to leave Paige in there to slip into a diabetic coma or worse. He nodded even as his frustration grew. "Yeah, I know."

A teenage girl was in imminent danger. The clock was running out for her. She couldn't afford to wait. If he messed this up, she could die.

Nash clapped him on the back. "Good luck."

Jake was going to need it. Crossing the street, he said, "You better hang back out of sight. Remember the conditions."

The powerful floodlights on Seventh had been shut off like he'd ordered.

Spotting the open window, he ran over and peered in. The light was off, but he could make out that it was an office. From the grass he didn't see anyone inside. "Hello. This is Jake. Can anyone hear me?"

"We hear you," Mister said, hidden from view.

The door to the office was open and he suspected Mister was somewhere in the hallway, where the light was still on, staying out of sight.

"I've got the bullhorn," Jake said, holding it up. "The press will be ready to listen to whatever you have to say in two hours."

"Two hours? Who is going to be watching at two in the morning? Was that the idea? To make sure I had the smallest audience possible?"

"No, of course not."

"Then I'll talk to them in the morning. At nine sharp. When people are watching and eating their breakfast."

"Okay," Jake said.

Someone peeked around the doorjamb, keeping as much of his head concealed as possible.

"Open your jacket, so I can see if you have a gun."

Jake did as he asked, even lifting it and turning around in a full circle, so he could see no weapon was hidden behind his back. "I'm unarmed."

"Okay. Toss the bullhorn in. Then we'll send out the hostages that we agreed on."

"Not just yet." This was not the way he wanted to handle this, off the cuff, but he had no choice. "First, we need to make a change to the deal."

"I knew I shouldn't have trusted you! You're a part of the system. All of you are the same."

"No, you can trust me," Jake said, keen not to lose the strides he had made. "It's just that I've learned some important new information that you need to hear."

"Oh yeah? What's that?" Mister asked.

"Paige Pietsch has type 1 diabetes. She must be released."

"No way! I told you we were keeping her and Tyler until this was done. As leverage!"

"Believe me when I say that you do not want a high-profile hostage that has a high-risk illness on your hands. She requires insulin shots. Special food. Regular blood tests to check her glucose levels."

"You're lying!" Mister yelled. "You'd say anything to get her out."

"If I was saying this just to get her out, why wouldn't I be saying it about Tyler instead? The truth of the matter is that the mayor's son is a bigger prize. There's only one mayor, but there are six other people sitting on the council. You have to let Paige go. Because if you don't, what you call leverage will easily and quickly turn into a liability. If she dies because you refused to let her get proper medical care, the right food and medicine, nothing you say to the media will matter."

Jake was tempted to go on pleading his case, but experience had taught him a certain rhythm. His gut told him this was the right point to take a beat and listen.

Voices came from the hall. Two men arguing. The disagreement went from zero to a hundred, getting loud and heated.

It sounded as if Mister wanted to comply, but one of the other men had concerns. Was Mister's authority being challenged?

A change in whoever was in charge among the captors wouldn't bode well, but infighting among them worked in Jake's favor.

After about a minute, their voices dropped to a whisper and then the fighting stopped altogether. "All right," Mister said. "You can have Paige."

Jake exhaled a breath of relief. Not only was he going to get an additional hostage, but it looked as though Mister was still calling the shots from the inside. "Send out the hostages and give me proof of life of the others and then I will toss in the bullhorn."

One by one the kids were released. The first one out was a girl with light brown hair.

Jake asked each of them their names while he helped them scramble through the window. As the fourth teen approached him, he saw the resemblance to Becca in the eyes and fiery curls.

"Mason Walker?" Jake asked.

Nodding, the kid said, "Yeah, that's me." He climbed onto the desk.

Jake helped him through the window. Then he pointed toward the blue-and-white trailer. "Run there. Agents are waiting."

The kid looked back at the library, almost as if reluctant to leave, but he took off running across the street.

Next came the final teen to be handed over. Felicia Pietsch's daughter. With dark hair and light brown eyes, she was a mini-me of her mother but with softer features.

"Paige?" he asked, grasping her hand and helping her climb out.

"Yes," she said, with tears in her eyes. Her whole body trembled as he got her out through the window and set her down on the grass.

He hoped the shivering was from fear and not from hypoglycemia and the start of insulin shock.

Jake repeated the instructions he'd given the others. Turning to the window, he waited for the last hostage.

Becca.

Seconds later, someone shoved her into the doorway of the office. Their gazes met across the distance. Her eyes were wide with alarm. There was a gun pointed at her head.

Jake's heart seized. "What's going on?" he asked.

"We're keeping the pregnant woman, but here's your proof of life."

Shock rocked Jake to the core. It was worse than being struck by a bolt of lightning. More damaging. At this critical moment, his attention was divided. His focus scattered.

"No." For a second, he was speechless, his heart struggling to beat. "You agreed to let her go."

"We're changing our end of the deal, also. Since we just gave you Paige, we're keeping the pregnant lady."

A deep pain ripped through Jake. "She's high-risk, too. It's better to let her go."

"I'm done negotiating for now. Those kids can verify that everyone else is alive and well. Throw in the bullhorn."

Jake didn't want to do it. If he gave them the bullhorn, any sway he had in getting her released now would be gone. They would just drag her out of sight, and he might never see her again.

He stared at Becca, the thought of leaving her there tearing him apart. Even though she trembled with the muzzle of a gun pressed to her temple, there was a fire ablaze in her eyes. She hadn't lost the will to fight.

But he needed to do or say something to get her free. He was so close to getting her out of there. Too close to give up.

"Release the woman also," Jake said, "or I'll shut off the water to the building and cut the power. Let her go and I'll send in some food. How about a few pizzas? You must be getting hungry by now."

"I said I'm done making deals for the night. You do whatever you have to, but we're keep her."

The thought of walking away from that building without Becca, when he could see her a few feet away, had pressure building in his chest.

She was steely and strong and had a take-no-prisoners attitude that annoyed him and attracted him at the same time. That was the thing she needed most. It would get her through this.

Still, there had to be some tactic he could use in this moment, but he couldn't think of anything.

"Throw it now!" Mister demanded. "Or there will be consequences for reneging on the deal."

Jake mouthed the words *I'm sorry*, to her.

A grim smile tugged at her mouth, and she gave him a slight nod that spoke volumes. She understood what he had to do.

Nonetheless, his heart squeezed as he tossed the bullhorn through the window.

"Back away, slowly," Mister said. "Tell those reporters to get ready to hear what I've got to say."

Each step Jake took was gut-wrenching, taking him

farther and farther away from Becca. He kept his gaze locked on hers, hating himself for failing to get her out when he had the chance.

Once he was in the middle of the street, someone shoved Becca forward. She stumbled, bent down and picked up the bullhorn.

He heard someone yelling at her to hurry up and get back as they beckoned to her with a waving gun. Without turning around or looking away from him, she eased back out of the room into the hall. A large hand snatched her by the arm, and she was yanked out of sight.

Spinning on his heel, Jake clenched his hands and ran around to the other side of the trailer.

Two ambulances were there, paramedics checking everyone out. Parents wrapped their arms around their children and held them close.

Clare Walker, Becca's sister, was crying as she buried her face in her son's hair and kissed his head. She had the same brown eyes and auburn curls. Tim hugged his family, holding tight to his son and wife. The gratitude on his face was almost too much to bear.

It hadn't been a complete failure, but...

"Where's Becca?" Nash asked him.

Jake shook his head. "They decided to keep her because they released Paige instead."

Nash's face grew somber, the regret in his eyes was clear. "We'll get her back," he said, his voice low but firm. "*You'll* get her back. Yeah?"

"Yeah," Jake said, his voice lacking Nash's confidence.

Lynn came up beside him and put a hand on his shoulder. "Are you going to be all right?"

No. He felt hollow and powerless. Split down the middle. He wouldn't be all right until Becca and all the others were safe. "Don't worry about me. Those kids need you."

With his sister counseling them, those teens might not be scarred from this for the rest of their lives. The sooner they spoke to a professional the better.

"We need to debrief the kids. Then Dr. Delgado should speak with your children before you leave," Nash said. "It's crucial to their mental well-being." Nash turned to the councilwoman. "Ms. Pietsch, we've got the EMTs standing by ready to examine your daughter to make sure she's all right. If necessary, they can rush her to the hospital for an insulin shot."

"Why would I need a shot of insulin?" Paige asked, looking between Nash and her mother.

Confusion washed over Jake. "For your type 1 diabetes," he said.

"She looks fine right now." Ms. Pietsch curled a protective arm around her daughter. "We should get you home, darling." She tried to pull her daughter away. "We'll make an appointment, Dr. Delgado."

Shaking her head as she was dragged along by the councilwoman, Paige said, "I don't understand. I don't have diabetes. My sister Penelope does." She stopped walking and looked at her mother. "What are they talking about?"

Councilwoman Pietsch sighed.

Jake stared at her, stunned that she would sink so low as to deceive federal agents. "You lied about your daughter having a life-threatening medical condition?"

Not only had she lied, but she had given elaborate details on the spot, ensuring that they swallowed the lie she had spoon-fed them.

Without a hint of remorse or the tears she had easily shed earlier, she straightened. "So what if I did?"

"They were going to release a woman who's pregnant." Anger rose in Jake like a tidal wave. "Her life and that of her unborn child matter, too."

"Are you a father, Agent Delgado?" Councilwoman Pietsch asked.

Not yet.

He thought of the gun pointed at Becca's head. A part of him wondered if he ever would be. "No. I'm not."

"Then you couldn't possibly understand my position. A parent will do anything to protect their child. Even lie. You should be thanking me," she said. "Instead of getting four minors out, you saved five." She took her daughter's arm and began walking away.

"Wait, Mom." Pulling away from her mother, Paige glanced at Nash and Jake. "There's something you guys should know. Mason's aunt has my cell phone. Those men took everyone else's, but she hid mine in her boot. It's on silent. But if they find it, they'll be so angry. The leader caught her spying on them earlier and one of his guys beat her for it." The girl wrapped her arms around herself and shivered. "He hit her so hard. Oh, God, that awful sound. He hit more than once until one of them made him stop because she's pregnant. But I don't know what they'll do to her if they catch her with my phone."

Chapter Seven

Inside the mobile command center, Jake paced, his anxiety churning.

"You're going to wear a hole in the floor," Lynn said.

They were alone in the trailer. Nash was busy handling the mayor before he called it a night. The kids were being examined by the EMTs and debriefed by Rocco. Due to the late hour, Lynn had spoken with them briefly. Tomorrow, she would give each teenager proper, individual counseling.

His sister patted the chair beside her. "Sit down for a minute."

He dropped into the chair. Not sure what to do with himself, he clenched and unclenched his hands, wanting to hurt the man who had hit Becca.

"Do you want to talk about it?" she asked, softly.

"Talk about what?"

"The fact that Becca is pregnant. I'm guessing it's yours."

"No," he said. Propping his elbows on his thighs, he dropped his head into his hands.

"It's not yours?" Surprise rang in her voice.

"No, it's mine. I just don't want to talk about it." Remembering the look on Becca's face when he had asked her whether the child that she was carrying was his sent a pang coursing through his chest. His sister put a comforting hand on his back. "Lola, I almost had her. I came so close to getting her out and I ended up leaving her behind."

"It came down to Paige or Becca. It was a tough call, but you made the right one. Becca is a highly trained agent. She can handle herself in there. You've got a ringer in there. I'd say that gives you a distinct advantage."

That was true. Having an agent in there spying, assessing weaknesses might give them the upper hand they needed. Those men would look at Becca and assume one thing based on her appearance, not realizing who they were really dealing with. A formidable opponent.

But it didn't make him feel any better. "Still, I should have been able to do more."

"You will. First, decompress and clear your head. I'll have Nash make sure that no one comes in for a few minutes. Then you're going to eat something."

"I'm not hungry."

"Hunger doesn't matter." She stroked his hair like he used to do to her when they were kids. "Nash taught me that. You have to keep up your strength. Eat and then get some rest. Doctor's orders."

"You're not that kind of doctor."

A sad chuckle left her lips. "I can't believe I'm going to be an auntie."

He still couldn't believe he might be a father…if he could get Becca out unharmed.

"You're better at keeping secrets than I realized," she said, her tone gentle, not reproachful. "You could've told me that you two were dating. Nash and I would've kept it quiet. You're both consenting adults."

Jake would have told her if they had in fact been dating. The truth was they hadn't been. No dinners. No movies.

Sometimes, as he held her in bed, they talked in the darkness. Sharing snippets, scraps of their lives. Filling in the quiet spaces. Nothing heavy. Nothing too deep. He didn't think it meant anything.

He hadn't wanted to label it.

Labels came with expectations and pressure. It was easier to say nothing at all.

"You're doing good," she said. "Terrific, actually, considering the stress you're under personally and from the mayor and Mr. Guidry. You can do this. You'll get her and the others out of there." His younger sister stood. "I'm going home. I need to rest and so do you. Where are you going to sleep tonight? Do you want to stay with me and Nash?"

He'd made sensational strides with Nash, but he didn't want to sleep under the same roof as him and his sister. Aaron had a room at the local B and B.

Jake's gaze slid to Becca's things. Her purse and keys. "No," he said. "There's a cot tucked away in the back that I'll pull out and get some shut-eye on. First, I think I'll go to Becca's. Shower. Change. Grab some things for her. As soon as she's released, she'll want toiletries and some fresh clothes." He had to stay positive. Hopeful.

"Okay. I'll see you in the morning. I plan to be here when the hostage takers make their statement and will meet with the kids later in the day. Hey, I know it will be hard, but you really do need to sleep." Lynn left the trailer.

He was grateful to have her support during all this.

Needing a few minutes to process everything before he faced anyone else out there, Jake ducked into the tiny bathroom of the mobile unit and leaned over the sink. Most of the mobile unit was outfitted in muted grays and shiny chrome. Normally the austere finishings helped to ground him. Now it felt cold and harsh.

Being alone with his thoughts was a blessing and a curse. A reprieve from the mayor. From the pointing of fingers and accusations. From the lies of desperate parents. But it was also an opportunity for him to reflect on his missteps that might cost Becca dearly.

He couldn't shake the uneasy, sick feeling settling in his chest. Those men had hit Becca. Several times. They had beaten her. He slammed his eyes shut, thinking about the way that poor girl, Paige, had shivered as she had told him about it.

His renewed anger tangled with dread. When Becca had the chance, she would use the phone. Because that was who she was and what she did. Took big risks, never playing it safe. She couldn't flip a switch and shut off being an agent, suppress the instincts that made her great.

It took a special kind of a woman to not only work

in a male-dominated field but to succeed in it as well. Becca was extraordinary. Stubborn as a mule and sexy as hell.

She wouldn't play by their rules.

And that was what worried him.

Guilt twisted through Jake like a noose. His fingers tightening around the edge of the sink, he stared at himself in the mirror.

Becca.

She was counting on him, but he couldn't brood over only her. He had to regain control and concentrate on getting all the others released. Keeping his emotions in check was imperative to do his job right. Vowing not to let down any of the hostages, he hitched up his resolve.

His cell vibrated.

Jake pulled the phone from his pocket. He glanced at the screen. His breath stalled in his chest. It was the number that Paige had given him before she'd left the area with her deceitful mother.

He answered before the second ring had finished, "Becca."

"Jake," she whispered, and he squeezed his eyes shut at the sound of her sweet voice.

"Are you all right?" he asked, all thoughts of how focusing on her was a distraction evaporated. "Is it safe for you to use the phone?"

"Listen to me. I don't know how much time I have," she said so low it was hard to hear her. "I'm sending you some pictures of the gunmen without their masks. The one in charge, Mister, and one of an older guy. I think they're friends. They're definitely the more lev-elheaded ones of the bunch."

His phone chimed at the incoming text message, but he didn't bother to glance at it just yet. "You shouldn't take such chances." Paige's words rang in his ears. He didn't want Becca to suffer any consequences.

"Have you been able to identify them?" she asked. "Anything on forensics?"

"No. Not yet." His fingers were crossed that Rocco would come through. He'd gladly give the guy a big, fat thank-you.

"Then I had to take the risk," she insisted. "I won't stop doing what I can from in here." The determination in her voice was unwavering.

"Do they know that you're FBI?" he asked.

"No."

Good. The longer she could keep them from find-ing out, the better. Once they realized, she'd become an even higher-value bargaining chip and known threat they'd keep a closer eye on. "You're one of the smartest, gutsiest agents I know. You've shown time and again that you're a hero. You don't have anything to prove—don't take any chances now."

"What? Are you kidding me?" Her frustration reso-nated clear as a bell over the line, and the last thing he wanted was to upset her. "If I were a man, if it was Nash or Rocco or any other male agent in here, you wouldn't say that to him."

Was it true?

Was he guilty of being sexist?

He only wanted to protect her, keep her safe. "I'm

sorry. Maybe you're right." Stifling a groan, he pulled the phone away from his ear a second. On the screen the video icon was illuminated. That meant their phones were compatible. They could do the equivalent of Face-Time, but on the Androids. "I'm going to try the video." He tapped the icon.

His face popped up first in the lower right corner of the screen.

Then Becca's in the center.

His heart clenched so hard he could barely draw a breath. He hadn't been able to see her well from the hallway of the library through the window. Now relief bloomed hot in his chest as he soaked in the sight of her.

She was pale with deep exhaustion in her eyes. There was a bright, fiery red mark on her cheek, a bruise forming, and a cut on her bottom lip.

He wanted to kill, with his bare hands, the man who had done that to her.

"Paige told me that one of the men beat you. Are you badly hurt?" he asked, a flare of anger lighting deep inside.

"No." She shook her head. "It was nothing," she said.

It was not nothing to him. One of the HTs had put his hands on an unarmed woman.

His woman.

His?

Was that what he wanted?

He only knew that he needed her to be safe and that whoever had hit her was a pathetic coward. Jake would make him regret the day he had ever laid a finger on her, if he got the chance.

"I'm okay. He slapped me a couple of times," she said, like it was no big deal. "The stocky guy with the black paisley mask. I found out his first name. One of the gunmen called him Craig. I saw his face, but I didn't get a picture of it. He's around his late thirties. White male. Has a mustache and a tattoo of a black spider on his left hand between his pointer finger and thumb. Mister told me something personal about him. That he has a problem with women. Went to therapy for it. But that he's incurable."

She had given him a lot to go on. They would be able to figure out the identity of at least one of the assailants. Once they did, it would be like dominoes falling, leading them to the rest.

"You did good," he said, wanting to hold her, kiss her, just to have her safe in his arms. "But you need to be careful. I mean, don't take any more unnecessary risks."

"What I'm doing isn't unnecessary. It's essential and you know it."

He could see her playing out various scenarios in her head and realized this was an argument he wasn't going to win. Because she was right.

But he didn't want her endangering herself. Or the baby.

"Promise me," he pleaded with her, "that you'll be careful."

"I will. Please trust my judgment for once."

Ever since the academy at Quantico, when they were put through a training exercise designed to test their problem-solving skills as well as their character in a no-win scenario, he had questioned her judgment. She had saved the pretend victims, but she hadn't survived the exercise.

That was the day he had learned that Rebecca Hammond wouldn't hesitate to sacrifice herself if meant saving the lives of others.

He loved that about her. She was everything he wanted in a woman, shrewd, bold, with so much fire in her brown eyes that it made his blood go hot at the challenge she embodied.

It was also what terrified him. He never wanted to get that phone call, another agent informing him that something had happened to her.

The kind of strength she carried she had earned the hard way, he suspected. He often wondered what she had gone through to gain that kind of resiliency.

"I trust you." And he did. He trusted her with his life.

He only wanted to be able to trust her to protect her own, too.

Becca glanced away like she was checking that no one was coming. "I found out more about them. Mister claims that they don't want to hurt anyone."

"I don't believe that," Jake scoffed, "if he's letting his men rough you up."

"No, it wasn't like that. I threw the first blow, after he grabbed me by the hair," she said, and somehow that didn't surprise him. "The altercation angered the one in charge. He made Craig stop. For some reason, I do believe him. If he can achieve his goal without killing anybody, I think that's how he'd prefer it."

Nice to hear, but he wasn't going to rely on the good-will of a criminal.

"They seized a library and took hostages, armed to the teeth," he said, unconvinced. Why so many weapons, popping off rounds of bullets, if they weren't prepared to hurt people?

"I know. Mister said something about needing to use extreme measures when taking on a powerful enemy."

What did that mean?

"Did he say what kind of enemy?" Jake asked. "Is it the system? An organization? A person?"

"I don't know. I'll try to find out more."

God, he wished she were more afraid. Fear would make her cautious and help keep her alive. "It's better if you don't. You've given me a lead. Let me do my job. Your whole team is working on this."

A sad smile pulled at her mouth. "Of course, they are."

"All you need to do is stay as safe as possible until I can get everyone released. I'll do whatever is necessary to get you out of there."

"I know you will. You're the best."

This was the one time he would give anything to rise to the expectations of his reputation. It was a lot to live up to. A lot for someone to be. More so when it came to people in his life.

He had believed they could have carried on casually, indefinitely, with neither risking the pain of getting their hearts involved.

What a fool he'd been.

Every time they'd slept together, things between them

had shifted like quicksand beneath his feet, sucking him deeper. He had sensed the growing affection, the intensifying ease of being with one another, the flourishing trust bred from familiarity. It was in the way she touched him, kissed him, made love to him. And it hadn't been one-sided. The passion ignited faster between them, burning hotter, until he forgot they were ever two separate people.

He had just been able to lock away the emotions and not dwell on it until now. Faced with the prospect of dealing with what he feared most.

Losing her.

And now their unborn child.

He wanted her, he wanted all the hostages, set free from whatever deadly game those lowlifes were playing. "Is there anything else about them that you can remember?"

"They're prepared to stick this out for a while. I take it they had planned on you shutting off the water at some point because they brought their own along with food."

The likelihood of hostages being released unharmed increased the longer they went without the basic human needs of food, water and sleep. But this was the first time he had encountered anyone preparing for it.

They had probably also anticipated that Jake might cut the power as well. Nonetheless, he had to follow through with it, though the impact to them would be minimal tonight. Tomorrow, they'd run low on food and eventually water. There would also be the heat to contend with. No air conditioning meant everyone in that building was going to bake. Including Becca.

"Around one in the morning, the power and water will be shut off. It's going to get hot in there."

With a brave face, she said, "I understand."

"If you find out anything else, don't get caught using the phone."

"I've got a low battery and no way to charge it. I might only be able to make one more call. I won't dare try unless I learn something vital." Her eyes registered alarm, her head whipping to the side. "I think someone is coming."

Her face disappeared as the line disconnected, the screen going dark.

And a gaping hole opened inside his chest.

BECCA BARELY HAD time to power down the phone and slide the cell into her boot before Craig unlocked and opened the door. He prowled into the room, face covered, with a duffel bag slung over his shoulder.

Staring at her, he narrowed his beady eyes. "Who were you talking to?"

Her heart beat like a snare drum. Had he heard her? "No one. I was singing to myself. I'm lonely. And scared." The last part was true.

She was scared, even though she was doing her best not to show it to anyone. Especially not to Jake, who was underestimating her yet again. She had never let fear hold her back before, and she would not now.

"Singing, huh?" he stepped closer, glaring at her with cold, hard suspicion.

She lowered her eyes and forced herself to shiver,

hoping her display of submissiveness would appease him. Hoping he would believe the lie she'd just told.

"You were told to be quiet. Don't let me hear you again."

"Okay. I'm sorry."

He stepped closer. "Come on. Get up."

Tension threaded through her. "Where are you taking me?" she asked.

"Back to the room with the others."

She exhaled a shuddery breath of relief and stood.

Craig cut the fresh zip tie they had put on her after handing her over didn't pan out. "The boss says you get to sleep unrestrained. Mess up, do something stupid again, and I'll take great pleasure in hog-tying you."

She didn't doubt him.

Snatching hold of her arm, he squeezed unnecessarily tight and escorted her to the story time room. After unlocking it, he shoved her inside.

She went over to the wall and sat in between Abigail and the mayor's son.

Craig opened the duffel. Then he tossed each of them a mini eight-ounce bottle of water and a snack size bag of pretzels. "Hang on to your bottles. We'll let you refill them at the fountain later if they haven't shut off the water by then." He closed the door and walked away.

"Are you all right?" Abigail asked her. "Did they hurt you?"

"No." Becca smiled at the older woman, not wanting her to worry. "I'm okay."

Relief washed over Abigail's face. "That's good." She patted Becca's arm. "You've got to do what they say.

Don't cause any trouble. You're so young. You have your whole life ahead of you. I don't want to see anything bad happen to you."

Neither did Becca, but she wasn't thinking about herself. Her concern was for the other hostages and the baby she was carrying. Somehow, she had to balance it all without getting hurt.

"You better drink and eat up, honey," Abigail said, gesturing to the food and water. "Dehydration can lead to serious health problems for a pregnant woman. Neural tube defects. Low amniotic fluid. Premature labor."

The litany of potential complications made Becca's head spin. She was no expert. Only yesterday had she ordered a pregnancy book online, but she was aware that proper hydration and nutrition were paramount.

As she opened the bottle of water, she realized was parched. Her mouth was dry and her throat a little sore. She took a long gulp.

"Better, right?" Abigail asked.

The cool water soothed Becca's throat, instantly giving her a little boost of energy. She nodded. They sat in silence for a bit. The minutes ticked by, getting closer to the approaching darkness when the power would be cut. She gathered her thoughts and her strength as she slowly savored her bag of pretzels.

In the corner, she overheard Nolan and Cameron talking softly.

"What do you do for fun?" the librarian asked.

"Teach. Read. Run," Nolan said. "I love to run. What about you?"

"Play the piano. I started when I was five. My mother

wanted me to be a concert pianist. I wasn't good enough. But I still love to play. This will be the first day that I haven't in over twenty-five years."

Abigail turned to Becca. "How far along are you?"

Her upcoming appointment with her doctor to find out was on Tuesday. "About eight weeks," she said, estimating based on when she and Jake last had unprotected sex.

Looking back on it, she had thought nothing of it—not using a condom. Actually, she hadn't been thinking at all. She'd been too swept up in kissing him until neither of them could barely breathe, in the smell of him, the feel of his skin against hers. That rush of something warm and sweet and thick, like sun-soaked honey, flowing in her veins. And afterward, she'd mistaken their impetuous act of carelessness for passion. As a sign that their fling had taken a step to something new. To the next level, of deep trust and intimacy beyond the physical.

Idiot. She'd been so stupid.

"Do you get morning sickness?" Abigail asked. "I had it with my first two."

"It's been pretty awful." Thanks to the nausea that lasted until late afternoon, she hadn't had much of anything to eat that day or to drink. Once it had passed, she'd been too anxious about seeing Jake.

When they had first met at Quantico, there had been an immediate attraction. He had movie star looks. Devastating features. Light brown skin the color of wet sand. Soulful hazel eyes. And a hot bod. He also consistently came in at the top of their class. Then they would have a moment to themselves away from the other cadets, and he would ruin it by opening his mouth.

Age had mellowed him out a bit. Refined his good looks. Made his appeal irresistible.

Becca had encountered a few old school macho types who didn't believe women belonged in law enforcement. Jake wasn't one of them. Deep down she didn't think he was sexist. It was just something about her that made his protective instincts flare hot.

From their first kiss in the parking lot of Delgado's—when she'd had that primitive, immediate, carnal response to him—she'd known. This would be different. Special. And that it was going to be hard as hell to walk away from him because no one had ever made her heart and body light up the way he did.

She guessed the only special thing to come out of this was the life growing inside her.

Maybe she needed to play her role as hostage a little safer. Jake might not want anything serious with her or to have a family together, but she wanted this baby. His child. She had to do what she could to protect it.

The gunmen turned on a couple of ultrabright lanterns that most likely ran on batteries.

They had been prepared to lose power as well.

Who were these guys? What did they want? And how far were they prepared to go to get it?

"Here, honey," Abigail said, offering her bag of pretzels. "You need it more than I do."

Becca was still starving and a mother-to-be, but she couldn't take it. "Thank you, but we don't know when or if they'll give us more food. You should keep it."

"Take a few of mine. You need the sustenance." Abigail opened her bag and poured some into her hand. "I won't eat the whole thing. Besides, my granddaughter keeps telling me that intermittent fasting would be good for me."

It was sweet of her. "Thanks." Pretzels and crackers were the two things she craved the most that she could keep down.

The lights in the building went out, plunging them into darkness. Then the air conditioning rattled and chugged, slowing down until it stopped completely.

"What's happening?" Cameron Lund asked.

Becca popped another pretzel in her mouth. "I think the authorities shut off the power."

"Wonderful," Nolan said. "I hope the water is still on. Otherwise, the toilets will only get one flush."

"At least we're not strapped to chairs with no hope of using the restroom, like the others," Becca said.

"It's supposed to be a record-breaking scorcher tomorrow. I doubt those thugs will open windows to let in fresh air," Nolan said, continuing to be a beacon of positivity. "It'll get much hotter in here than outside. The cops, or the FBI, or whoever is in charge out there had better get us released before noon. Otherwise, we'll have to worry about heat stroke and turning into scrambled eggs as well as the possibility of getting shot."

Blocking out Nolan's dark thoughts, Becca said, "I'm sure the authorities are doing their best."

"I hope so," Abigail chimed in. "You're more likely to get heat stroke sooner than the rest of us because you're pregnant. It won't be good for you or the baby."

Putting a hand to her belly, Becca knew this process couldn't be rushed, but she prayed Jake was able to work out some kind of miracle before she had to deal with oppressive heat that might harm their child.

IT WAS AFTER two in the morning when Jake unlocked the door to Becca's home using her key. Her condo was in a complex close to the edge of town. Her place was sparse but comfortable. Homey and warm.

He liked that she didn't need to overstuff her life with unnecessary things. What was most important to her was front and center. Family. Pictures of them were everywhere. She was in some, smiling so bright it radiated in her eyes, kissing her nephew, fishing and riding horses together with her sister and in-laws.

Walking through the apartment, he found the faint smell of her perfume lingering in the air. Peonies mixed with something else he couldn't identify. In the kitchen, he could almost hear her laughing and talking about a case as she sipped a beer.

Her presence was there, surrounding him, even though she was trapped in that library. There was also an emptiness that permeated the condo.

He kicked off his boots and trudged into the bedroom. His shoulders ached with residual tension. Dropping onto the bed, he lay down on top of the covers. He grabbed a pillow from her side and held it to his nose, inhaling her feminine scent.

Too many moments they'd shared in this room, in this bed, that he had taken for granted. Simply assuming there would be more. Not fully appreciating how in the past he had been with others, yet only this one woman was capable of reeling him back.

The thought of never seeing Becca again sent a new ache cutting through him like a knife. The ferocious need to keep her safe, to be near her, was overwhelming.

He needed to get it together.

Opening the top drawer of the nightstand, he removed a pad and pencil. He replayed his conversation with her, going through the details again.

Before he had left the command center, he'd already written a report for the team and uploaded the pictures Becca had sent into the system. Aaron had started running the photos through the database in search of matches, but the process would take hours. In the meantime, Aaron was getting some rest, too, in the B and B.

If there were any new developments inside the library while Jake was gone for a bit, a deputy would call him.

He circled certain things on the notepad that had all been in his report. Now, in the quiet of her apartment, it was easier for him to focus, connecting the dots.

Craig. Mustache. Tattoo of a black spider. A problem with women. Therapy. Incurable.

Lynn would be able to help. She was already asleep and couldn't reach out to local clinics until later. First thing in the morning, he needed to talk to his sister.

Chapter Eight

Parking in front of the Compassionate Hearts charity, Brian noticed a gated lot to the side of the building. Inside were three late-model sedans that had seen better days.

He slipped on his cowboy hat and strode up to the door. The sign posted read that they didn't open until ten, but he saw movement inside. He tried the door. It was open, so he went in.

Two young women were busy working, sorting through clothes and hanging them up.

The older, more attractive of the two looked up from a clothing rack where she was putting price tags on various items. "I'm sorry," she said with a warm smile, "but we're not open yet."

With curly blond hair braided into pigtails that made her look like Goldilocks, she appeared younger than she probably was. He estimated she was about thirty. The other lady was closer to midtwenties.

Holding up his badge, he said, "I'm Detective Brian Bradshaw." He returned the grin. Blondes were his weakness. "I'm investigating the theft of two vehicles. Who can I talk to about that?"

Her smile faded. "It's good that you're here." She wore a Compassionate Hearts T-shirt and jeans that showed off her petite figure. No name tag. "Mrs. Martinez has been a wreck about it. You can head on back to the office. She's in there."

He tipped his hat in thanks to her and headed down the aisle in between clothing racks. Glancing back over his shoulder for one more look at Goldilocks, he caught her watching him. An embarrassed smile spread across her pretty face, making his grin grow wider.

Only two things were stopping him from asking her out for a cup of coffee or to lunch. One, he didn't hit on women while he was working, which seemed like all the time and explained why he was habitually single. Two, no one compared to Charlie Sharp. Every lady he was interested in he'd inevitably compared to her, in looks, temperament and prowess.

Not only did he have a thing for blondes, but he guessed he liked his women beautiful, mean and deadly.

Charlie was all the above.

"Excuse me," Brian knocked on the open door, making the brunette seated behind the desk jump. "Didn't mean to startle you, ma'am. I'm Detective Bradshaw, with the Laramie PD. I had a few questions about the two vans that were stolen."

"Oh, I didn't think they'd send anybody over." She stood, proffering her hand. "I'm Aleida Martinez. Thank you for coming," she said as they shook. "I felt like you guys couldn't have cared less."

"Sorry about that. If you don't mind me asking, what gave you that impression?"

"Once the officer learned that it was a couple of vans from our lot, where we keep the vehicles donated to charity that we plan to auction, it was like he completely shut down. A part of me gets it. We're only going to get a few hundred bucks from the sale, but every dollar counts to us."

"I understand," Brian said, keeping his tone sympathetic. "When did you notice the vans were missing?"

"As soon as I arrived yesterday morning," she said, her voice going higher with alarm. "I don't know if you noticed, but we don't have many out there to auction. Two missing vans stood out."

"But they were there when you closed up the night before?" he asked.

"Yes, Detective." Nodding, she glanced out the window toward the lot. "I'm always the last one to leave. I had worked late to file some paperwork. On my way out, I checked the lot."

"Do you keep it locked?"

"I do."

"And it was locked when you left?" he wondered.

She hesitated. "I think so. I saw the padlock on."

"Had either the gate or the lock been cut?"

"Yes," she said. "The lock."

"Do you happen to have any security footage?" he asked.

Mrs. Martinez frowned. "As if we can afford that. We've never had an issue before with anyone breaking into the store or the lot. Everyone in town knows we're struggling to help others. That's why this is so disturbing."

"Well," Brian said, "the two stolen vans are currently evidence in an ongoing investigation."

"They were used to commit a crime?" she asked, sounding surprised.

"Afraid so."

Sitting down, she shook her head. "What is this world coming to?"

"When did you receive the vans?" he asked.

"Three days ago."

They hadn't been on the lot long. "Did you know the vans were coming? Was the delivery coordinated in advance?" Maybe an employee knew where someone could steal two vans that the cops wouldn't care about.

"No, we get donations unexpectedly," Mrs. Martinez said. "Although once a year, we usually get one or two from the Plainsman Oil and Gas Company. I believe they map out which ones will be donated in advance because they base it off the mileage on the vehicle."

"Is that who donated the two vans?" he asked.

"Yes, it was. They're very generous."

Adding the details to his notes, Brian said, "Did the drivers have to sign anything when they dropped them off? Complete any paperwork?"

"No. That's not how it works. The day I'm going to receive a vehicle from them, I'll get an email from the transportation department notifying me," she said. "The drivers just turn over the keys and title. Within thirty days of the sale of the vehicles, I send their headquarters written acknowledgement and a receipt that will have the gross selling price, year, make, model and vehicle

identification number. I send the company paperwork after the vehicles are sold."

"You mentioned *keys*." His mind snagging on the fact there had been more than one. "How many sets do you get from the oil company?"

She hesitated for a moment, thinking. "Usually two."

"Usually? How many did you get to each van the last time?" he asked.

"Only one key. It had been a hectic afternoon when they were delivered. I guess I didn't think much of it."

Brian nodded, taking notes. "Do you have a point of contact over at the Plainsman Oil and Gas Company?"

"Yes. It's the head of their transportation department. Dennis McKee."

AFTER GETTING THE runaround at the Plainsman Oil and Gas Company headquarters, Brian had finally made his way to the transportation department, which was located on a remote site, out in the boonies. It was closer to where the company did all their drilling and fracking. Rigs pumping crude oil were dotted across the land.

At a little guard shack, he flashed his badge at security. "I'm Detective Bradshaw. I need to speak with Dennis McKee, regarding two of your company vans that were used in an ongoing crime."

The security guard got on the phone and spoke to someone.

Brian glanced around at the chain-link fence and security cameras.

The guard hung up the phone. "Head over to the transportation department," he said, pointing to one

of several small buildings that was little more than a glorified trailer.

"Thanks." When the gate opened, Brian drove his truck over and parked in front of the building.

Putting on his cowboy hat as he hopped out, he spotted a fleet of other white vans, like the ones used by the men who had taken over the library, along with oil field trucks and a host of other vehicles parked near a large four-bay garage.

He opened the door and shut it behind him to keep out the summer heat. Catching the eye of the receptionist, he smiled. "Hi, there. I need to speak to the head of transportation," he said, holding up his badge.

The middle-aged woman hiked a thumb over her shoulder. "That would be Dennis McKee."

Tipping his hat in thanks, he strode across the trailer to the other desk.

"How can I help you, Detective?" Dennis said.

"There is currently a hostage situation over at the Laramie Public Library. The gunmen used two white vans originally belonging to the Plainsman Oil and Gas Company. They were stolen from the premises of the Compassionate Hearts charity. How far in advance do you schedule when and which vehicles will be donated?"

Dennis shrugged. "I don't know. It varies."

"Based on what?"

"Different factors. Mainly mileage."

Brian pulled a piece of paper from his pocket that had the vehicle identification numbers written on it and set it down on the desk. "Can you check for me regarding these?"

Dennis looked over the paper. "Do you have the license plate numbers?"

"No. I don't."

"That would've been the fastest way to verify when it was scheduled to be donated. Do you mind waiting a few minutes while I look into this?"

"Nope."

"Help yourself to some coffee."

Normally he didn't drink more than two cups a day. Today he'd already had three espressos before 7 a.m., but since this was looking as if it might be a grueling day, he figured he might as well power up.

Grabbing a paper cup, he poured some coffee and added a couple of packets of cream.

Dennis clacked away at his computer while Brian strolled around the trailer, doing his best to be patient. Halfway through his cup of joe, McKee said, "I've got something for you."

Brian strode closer. "I'm all ears."

"Apparently, I logged those two vehicles to be donated a month ago. Once our transportation vans hit eighty thousand miles, they're designated to be given to charity."

"Did the charity pick them up or were they delivered?" Brian asked, wanting to verify what Mrs. Martinez had told him.

"We always deliver them."

"Who were the drivers?"

Dennis shrugged. "I don't know," he said. "That's not the kind of thing I log and keep track of. Someone volunteers and takes it over"

"How many sets of keys do you keep for each van?"

"Two."

"Do you give the charity both sets?"

"Yup, sure do. Along with the title."

Someone with keys to the vehicles had helped the gunmen. The person was either linked to Compassionate Hearts or the Plainsman Oil and Gas Company. Right now, it was looking like the latter.

"Right." Nodding, Brian gave a small smile, hiding his frustration. "I'd like to see the security footage of the day the vehicles left the premises."

"Sure, no problem." Spinning to face his computer, Dennis typed away again. A minute later, he said, "Oh no." He gave a belabored sigh. "I take it back. That is going to be a problem. Sorry, but you can't."

Putting a fist on his hip, Brian asked, "Why not?"

Frowning, Dennis turned his monitor to where Brian could see it. "We've been having some issues with our security cameras recently. They were down for repairs for that day," he said, pointing out the date in question.

Something was off here. Way off.

The business downtown had declined to cooperate and hand over security footage that might have proved useful in getting a photo of a suspect. Now, here at the transportation department for the Plainsman Oil and Gas Company, the security cameras had been conveniently malfunctioning on the day the drivers could be identified.

"I really am sorry I couldn't be more helpful," Dennis said, bright-eyed and not sounding the least bit sincere. "Is there anything else I can do you for you? I'm

about to wrap up and head to headquarters for a meeting. They don't like it when I'm late."

"No," Brian said, trying not to sound as defeated as he felt. "There's nothing else."

His gut told him that Dennis or someone else here had arranged for the gunmen to get access to the vans. Until they got a positive ID on the hostage takers there was nothing more he could do here, and it bugged him because he was a big believer in following through and tying up loose ends.

He still needed to check with the owners of the vehicles whose license plates had been stolen, but it would have to wait until after he got back to the mobile command center to hear the lead unsub address the media.

He knew it was going to be something big.

Perhaps even crazy.

Either way, he wanted to be there to hear it firsthand.

BECCA HAD MANAGED a few hours of sleep. She'd dreamed about Jake and the baby. He'd been pushing a stroller as they walked through a park together. The sun had been bright and warm, shining down on them. The grass and leaves gleamed. For once, they had not been fighting. They'd been talking and laughing and sharing their hopes for a future together. She had seen such love in his eyes that it had brought tears to her own.

What a total fantasy.

The harsh reality was she was on her own. As usual. It was early morning, and while it was still cool outside, and it was already warm inside the library. Once the afternoon temperature reached its peak, this building was going to become an oven.

Becca rolled onto her knees and stood.

"What are you doing?" Abigail reached out, taking her hand, urging her back down.

"I've got to go to the bathroom." They all probably did, but since she'd been pregnant her bladder hadn't quite been the same.

"Let me get their attention," Abigail said. "I doubt they'd hit an old woman for asking. You on the other hand…" She shrugged.

Smiling, Becca gestured for her to go ahead. Not only was Abigail brave, but she was also kind.

Abigail climbed to her feet and stretched like she was stiff. She took tentative steps toward the large glass window and knocked on it. "Excuse me." She waved at someone.

A moment later, Craig approached the room.

"We need to you use the facilities, if you don't mind," Abigail said.

Nodding, Craig looked back over his shoulder. "They have to go to the bathroom," he bellowed. "Should I take them?"

"Yeah!" someone called out, presumably Gray.

Craig unlocked the door. "Women first. Then I'll come back for you three," he said, referring to Lund, Nolan and the Schroeder kid. He looked at Becca. "Let's get moving."

She stood. It was good to get up and stretch after sitting for so long, but she was keenly aware of how volatile the situation was. Craig struck her as the most dangerous.

The restroom wasn't far, only a few feet to the left.

On the way, she asked, "Will we get any food this morning? More water?"

Morning sickness hadn't kicked in yet, thankfully, but it would soon and then she wouldn't be able to eat. Water was a higher priority.

Craig nudged Becca forward. "Not if it means you'll need to keep running to the bathroom."

"She needs water and food." Abigail looked back at him with a supplicating expression on her face. "Because she's pregnant. Can you find it in your hearts to give her some?"

"We all need water and food." Becca was more concerned about the others than she was for herself. "Even those who have been tied up all night."

"Not my call," Craig said. "We'll see." He pushed open the bathroom door.

After Becca and Abigail entered, Craig followed them inside.

Stiffening in alarm, Becca turned to him. "I hope you don't intend to watch like some pervert?"

"Maybe I do." His eyes brightened like he was smiling under his mask. "But if you keep insulting me, I'm going to smack you again. This time Frank ain't here to help you."

Another name. *Frank.*

"Please." Abigail stepped in between them. "There are no windows in here. Nothing that that can be used as a weapon. Won't you be a gentleman and let us ladies use the bathroom with a little dignity?"

Craig grunted as he eyed Becca hard. Like he was aching for a chance to hit her.

Her pulse pounded. Her gut twisting into a knot, she itched to do damage to him as well.

"Fine," Craig said, never taking that maniacal stare off Becca. "Hurry up. Don't make me come back and check on you. Or you'll regret it." With a shove against the door, he left.

Becca steeled herself for what was to come between her and that man. Not right now, but it would happen. Something told her it was inevitable.

Before this was all over, they were going to reach a flash point.

Where only one of them would make it through alive.

THE DOOR TO the command center closed. Jake spun in his chair to see who had entered. Lynn strode toward him as Nash locked the door.

"Morning, everyone," she said.

Aaron waved hello without looking up from his computer screen.

His sister came up to him. "Did you get any rest?" Her tone was what he imagined she used with clients in therapy.

Jake shrugged a casual shoulder, even though tension radiated through him. He'd managed to get a little dreamless sleep after tossing and turning for hours on the cot, worried about Becca and the other hostages. Wondering if she was able to get any rest. "Enough to function."

"Well, that's something." She gave him an encouraging smile.

"I need to talk to both of you," Jake said. "Becca contacted me on the Pietsch kid's cell phone last night after you left."

"You talked to her?" Nash asked. "How's she holding up?"

"Hanging in there." She was one of the toughest women he knew. Scratch that, one of the toughest *agents,* and wouldn't wilt under pressure. He was privileged to know her. "She's been listening. Asking questions. There's a lot to share. I've written up a report with all the details. She managed to get pictures of two of the HTs—Mister and a guy with a blue neck gaiter. I've uploaded them to the system. Aaron is trying to work his magic."

Agent Vance was studiously at it. "I'm running the pictures through our facial recognition database," he said, from in front of his computer screen.

What he neglected to mention was that he also had access to an artificial intelligence program that scraped billions of images from the internet—Facebook, LinkedIn, YouTube, Instagram, Snapchat, TikTok, you name it.

Aaron sipped his coffee. "I'm also combing through DMV records."

"The odds are high we'll get matches for both," Jake said.

Nash nodded in agreement. "Becca did good."

No, she had done great, despite his warning for her to stop. Becca was clever, he'd give her that. Reckless but clever—and effective. Any inside information was useful, but it wasn't worth the risk if it jeopardized her. "I need something from you, Lynn."

"What's that?" his sister asked.

"The HT that hit Becca has a history of having issues with women. Apparently, he's been to therapy for it and was described as incurable. Can you reach out to all the local clinics to see if he was treated there?"

"Sure." Taking out her phone, Lynn sat down. "What else do we know about him?" She opened a note-taking app.

"White male. Dark eyes. Black hair." As soon as Becca had mentioned the black paisley face mask, he instantly knew which guy she was talking about. "Mid to late thirties," Jake said, and his sister began typing. "His first name is Craig. He has a thick mustache and a tattoo. Of a black spider."

"Where's the tat located?" Nash asked.

"Oh my God." With a look of disbelief on her face, Lynn shook her head. "The tattoo is on the back of his left hand. Here." She indicated the fleshy space between her thumb and pointer finger. "Isn't it?"

"Yeah." Jake nodded. "How do you know that?"

Lynn lowered her gaze. "I've counseled him. He's in my domestic violence program."

"Who is he?" Nash asked. "What's his full name?"

She looked up at him. "Craig Hicks."

Gotcha.

One down. Three to go.

THE HELICOPTERS THAT would have drowned out the sound of his voice had been pulled back as promised. Watching as the camera crews set up in the morning light just beyond the new cordons the authorities had hastily erected, Frank still didn't like this. Addressing the public in this way wasn't how he and Hannah had envisioned things playing out.

He thought he'd be sitting across from reporters from at least two rival networks to ensure the rich and powerful higher-ups didn't suppress the story. Because that was what the well-connected one-percenters did. Protected each other. Instead, he'd get his chance to take his time, doling out the pieces of their story slowly, like breadcrumbs, leading them down the yellow brick road. But most importantly, he had imagined speaking to the press in a composed, eloquent manner.

With dignity.

Frank refused to talk about his Marianne, lurking in the shadows, screaming out a damn window.

He wanted a chance to speak, deserved it after everything they had suffered, but… Not like this. Hiding from snipers. Not taken seriously.

Unseen.

Unheard.

Sure, they would hear the words he shouted from a bullhorn as if he were a common criminal, but no one would really be listening. Folks would tune in for a show, to see if he would be shot and killed, assuming they were crazed gunmen on a rampage.

What he wanted was an in-depth interview with a couple of big-time journalists. Top-notch reporters whom people respected. One of those prime-time specials that drew high ratings. People paid close attention and listened to those.

Pulling out his burner cell, he dialed Hannah's number. His goddaughter would know what to do. She didn't simply accept what she was given. Somehow, she managed to flip the script, doing something unexpected.

"Are you ready?" she asked. "They just announced on the news that the gunman in charge is going to make a statement in an hour."

He explained the terms and conditions under which he would be giving that statement. "I don't like it."

"What about using the laptop I gave you and reaching out to the press on Zoom?"

"Dale had an accident and dropped it. Cracked the screen. You can't see anything."

"What about using your phone? You could call into a station. Or I could help you download a Zoom app. You might be more comfortable with that than a bullhorn."

How long would it take to verify who he was? That he was in fact the man in charge of the hostage situation. Once they believed him, he still had to deal with all the technical stuff that, he was ashamed to admit, he wasn't very good at.

A bullhorn he knew how to operate. Zoom? He'd never been on it once in his life. Besides, he had no control over what one network would do having exclusive control over his story. He wanted multiple networks, owned by different people, to hear it at the same time.

Thankfully, Hannah had stopped pushing for him to upload his statement on to YouTube. His video would sit in a void with no way to predict if anyone would watch it. Or how many. Where was the nobility in that kind of gamble?

He was a baby boomer who preferred a physical newspaper over anything online.

The old-school way still worked for a reason. Carried more gravitas, too.

"I can manage the bullhorn better than I can download some app. The real problem is I wanted prime time when I made my first statement so that I would get more viewers than I will now. It needs to be aired across multiple networks."

"It's a good thing you didn't settle for two in the morning when no one would have been watching. Remember, this is just an opener. The first card in our hand that we're showing."

There were more cards to come. "I get that, but I can't read everything you wrote down through a bullhorn. That speech is way too long." She had written him a full page. A beautiful page, but the words were not meant to be delivered while screeching at people. "I need something short and sweet. Until I get the chance later to tell our full story my way." Come hell or high water he was going to get his sit-down interview. If not for his first statement, then for his final one. He just had to figure out how to make it happen without that agent, Jake Delgado, stopping it.

"Give me a minute," Hannah said. "I can help you with short and sweet."

Good, since it was the reason that he was calling.

His goddaughter was much more than a firebrand. She was his beacon. Guiding him through the darkness, clearing away the shadows that haunted him.

After Marianne died, depression had threatened to

swallow him whole. There had been many times when he was tempted to give up and join her in the grave. But it was Hannah who showed him that he had a choice.

He could be a quitter, acquiescing to evil.

Or he could be David. Taking on Goliath.

All he needed was the courage to see this through.

Seconds later, his phone chimed. "I sent you a text," Hannah said. "That's your new statement."

Frank opened the message and read it.

"What do you think?" she asked, in response to his silence, eagerness in her voice. "Do you like it? Will it work for you? Is it too on the nose? I can write something else."

He smiled. *That's my girl.* "This will do nicely as an opener. For sure, it'll get them all talking." It was perfect. "Hannah, once the hostages are eventually released, regardless of whether or not *he* complies with all our demands, that's your cue to act. Okay, honey. For Marianne."

His goddaughter was his ace in the hole.

"We'll take everything from *him*. One way or another. For Marianne."

REACHING THE COMMAND CENTER, Brian strode up to Nash and Jake, who were both standing outside next to the trailer. "Has it happened yet?" he asked.

"Nope. Just in time," Nash said. "Did you get a chance to read the Jake's report and look over the pictures he uploaded?"

"Not yet, but I asked Aaron to forward me a copy." They all faced the west side of the library, where the window had once again been opened. "I didn't learn anything helpful regarding the vans that were stolen from the lot of Compassionate Hearts. They were originally registered to an oil and gas company, who delivered them to the charity three days ago. A set of keys for each were missing. But getting security footage or the names of the drivers led to a dead end."

Nash turned to him, his mouth opening.

"Please, don't ask." Brian was sick of coming up short. "Something is off about this case, but I haven't been able to put my finger on it."

Jake caught his gaze. "Off in what way?"

"The lack of cooperation. The all too convenient explanations. How I keep coming up with nothing concrete. It's weird." The hair on the back of his neck rose, as he thought about it. "Anything new on your end?"

"We've got a name of one of the HTs," Jake said. "Craig Hicks. Aaron has pictures of two more and is combing the databases to find a match."

It was only a matter of time. In this day and age, it was impossible to hide your identity once the authorities had a picture of you unless you lived off the grid. Once that business downtown opened for the day, one of the deputies from the sheriff's department would serve the warrant and hopefully the team would get one more photo.

A squawk came from a bullhorn inside the library, stealing their attention.

"Hello," Mister said over the screech of feedback, hidden from sight. "I, um, I have prepared a statement for the press regarding our actions, which I am certain have been misconstrued and vilified." He cleared his throat and hesitated. "Not every criminal is a bad guy. Think of Robin Hood. A hero to some. An outlaw to others." His voice strengthened, his tone hardening. "Although we have taken hostages, *we* are not the bad guys. We have released children as proof. Sometimes those you hold in the highest regard are the true villain. We want six and a half million dollars. We do not expect hardworking taxpayers or even the FBI to come up with such an enormous sum. It is not their debt to settle. We only want one man to pay...for *all* his sins. Crispin Lund."

Chapter Nine

"Who is Crispin Lund?" Jake asked, looking at Nash and Brian. "I presume he's somehow related to Cameron Lund." One of the staff members being held hostage.

Choosing to take over the library suddenly made more sense.

"Damn it." Nash swore. "I bet Crispin Lund is his father. I knew he had an adult kid."

"But who exactly is he?" Jake wondered.

Nash held up a hand, gesturing for him to hold on. "Brian, go get Mr. and Mrs. Lund and bring them here before reporters swarm their house. Hurry."

Leaping into action, Brian took off without a word.

Nash turned, stalking back to the command center.

Jake was right beside him. "I need an explanation. Now." Not being from this town was suddenly presenting a disadvantage he didn't like.

"The Lunds are the richest, most powerful family in town. Crispin is an upstanding pillar of the community," Nash said. "More influential and potentially problematic than the mayor. He's got a lot of extended family in town, other Lunds that he's not close to. I didn't realize the librarian, Cameron, might be his son."

"I take it Crispin Lund has that kind of ransom money. Six and a half million dollars?" Jake asked.

"He does." Nash climbed the steps of the trailer, opened the door and went inside. "This whole time, it was all about money."

Following him in, Jake locked the mobile unit door behind him. He noticed that the snake, Guidry, had slithered back inside the command center. He sat in the back, out of the way, drinking coffee.

When their gazes collided, Guidry held up his hand, actually waving hello.

As if anyone in the trailer wanted to see him after the stunt he'd pulled.

Jake rolled his eyes, not interested in wasting time or energy on the jerk, who lacked the ability to be a good negotiator. All Jake knew was that Guidry had better have the sense to keep his mouth shut today.

"It doesn't add up," Jake said, and Nash stared at him with skepticism. "Yes, they asked for money."

"A lot of it."

Six and a half million. Why not simply six or round up to seven? That half, dangling there, irked Jake. "If this was only about getting ransom, they could've relayed it to me. To get the ball rolling faster. Captors interested in cash want it as quickly as possible. They don't drag things out waiting to make some big statement to the media. Becca told me the HTs believe they have to take these extreme measures because they're taking on a powerful enemy. Then they announce to the world that Crispin Lund needs to pay for his sins. My gut tells me this goes deeper."

Shaking his head, Nash looked to Lynn. "Any thoughts?"

"I read Jake's report along with Becca's insights and after listening to the kidnapper's statement, I'm inclined to agree with him. They clearly feel justified. They believe they're the Robin Hood."

"Yeah, but Hood stole from anyone who was rich to give to the poor. To him, being wealthy was a crime."

"Aaron," Jake said. "Play back the statement." He was certain the agent had recorded it. The replay began. They all listened intently while Jake jotted down notes. Once it was finished, he said, "They describe themselves as heroes. And Lund as the true villain. With a debt to settle."

"Not only that," Lynn said, "but the phrasing 'We only want one man to pay for all his sins.' Usually when a person wants someone to pay for their sins, they don't just mean literally, with money. I believe the use of such language may be figurative as well."

His jaw tightening, Nash still looked uncertain.

Lynn folded her arms. "The Powells are wealthy. No mention of them. This isn't just about socioeconomic status and rebalancing the scales. They didn't even ask for Schroeder to pay," she said, snatching Guidry's full attention, "and they have his son. A hostage they insisted on keeping."

They had insisted. But for what reason? They weren't targeting the mayor. So why not release his kid?

"Let's see if we're right." Jake picked up the phone,

dialed the private line to the library, and put the call on speaker.

"Hello," Mister said, answering on the third ring.

"This is Jake. That was some statement you made. Why were you afraid to tell me that directly?" he asked.

"I wasn't afraid. I just don't intend to be silenced, to have our grievances swept under the rug and forgotten. I want people to know who Crispin Lund really is and I want it on the record."

"What has he done to you?" Jake asked, hoping to get the guy talking.

"That man, Lund, knows full well and he's going to pay for it."

Raising his eyebrows, Nash made an expression as if to say, *See, I told you so*.

But Jake wasn't convinced. "Give me the account number where you want the money wired."

A pause. A long one. "Has Lund agreed to pay the money?"

"We haven't spoken to him yet, but we will shortly. He's on his way."

"That bastard is coming here?" Mister asked.

Nash stabbed the mute button. "Was it a mistake telling him? What if it drives him to do something rash?"

"What if it's the catalyst we need to find out what this is all about?" Jake unmuted the call. "Yes, he is."

Nash exhaled a harsh breath.

"Good," Mister said. "Tell him to get the money ready. I'm sure it'll take a day or two to make it happen. I'll give you the account number then. In the meantime, I want to talk to him."

Nash shook his head vehemently.

"Talk to him about what?" Jake asked.

"Never you mind. That's between him and the rest of us."

"Why did you seize the library?" Jake probed. "Was it to get to Cameron?"

"Yeah, that's right," Mister said, sounding smug.

"Would've been easier to snatch him from his house. Contact Lund directly," Jake said. The FBI still would've been brought in, but why the spectacle, the drama, the need for other hostages?

"Then the world wouldn't know the truth." Mister's tone turned somber. "And Crispin Lund simply would have hired someone to track us down and kill us without ever paying for his sins."

"What sins?" Jake asked. "What has he done?"

"Things he thought he could get away with," Mister said. "But we're here, in this library, to prove him wrong."

"Are you trying to protect yourselves by being in the library, with the media and the authorities watching? Do you think this is any safer?" Because it wasn't. There were SWAT snipers all around the building, willing and ready to take a shot.

"Safer?" Mister scoffed. "Hell no. Lund's people can get to us anywhere. Even in here. We're dead men walking, but not before we get what we're after."

Lynn's eyes flared wide.

Criminals who believed they had no chance of surviving the outcome were the most volatile. The most unpredictable. The most dangerous.

Those types of cases were also the most likely to end in failure to get the hostages out alive.

"And what are you after?" Jake needed him to spill his guts. Usually, rage made folks vent. "What are you hoping to achieve? Is it just about the money?"

"I'll tell Crispin myself. Call me when he gets there."

Glaring at Jake, Nash shook his head no once again, more forcefully.

Ignoring him, Jake fell back on his extensive training and his instincts, which had never led him astray. "If you want to talk to him, you'll have to release the hostages first."

"No." The tone in his voice brooked no argument.

But why? He only needed one hostage.

Cameron.

Why not release some more of the others?

"How about releasing a few of them?" Jake suggested. "Tyler Schroeder." To that, Guidry stood and nodded. "Rebecca Hammond. Abigail Abshire." None of them were being used as human shields in front of the doors. He had nothing to lose and something to gain. "A minor, a pregnant woman and a senior citizen. Let them go before it gets really hot in there. We'll send in food and water for you." The captors didn't need the last part, but they didn't know that Jake was aware of that.

"I said no. If you're worried about the heat, then turn the power back on. First, I talk to Lund. Then we'll see whether I let any others go. Don't call back unless he's there." Mister hung up, ending the discussion.

"Why would you agree to put Crispin Lund on the line with him?" Nash asked.

"Technically, I didn't agree." It was implied as part of a quid pro quo. "I asked for something in order to make that happen."

Worry evaporated from Nash's face. "Okay. Good," he said, with less strain in his tone. "You're not going to let him talk to Lund then?"

Crossing his arms, Jake leaned back in his chair. "No, I am."

"What? Why?" Nash demanded.

"Their grievance is with him. What they want in exchange for releasing the hostages can only come from him. Letting them speak while we're listening is the fastest way to get to the bottom of it. They didn't go to him directly because they've either already tried that or they're afraid to."

"Mister said that he's not afraid," Nash pointed out. "Maybe they're waiting for Lund to get on the phone to start killing hostages until they get what they want."

"I don't believe that's the case," Jake said, wishing he could offer something concrete to substantiate his conviction.

"Then why didn't they agree to release the kid, Abigail Abshire and Becca?"

There were still too many missing pieces of the puzzle, leaving Jake in the dark. He didn't have an answer.

"Professional opinion," Nash said, looking at Lynn. "Are those gunmen psychopaths with no clear understanding of the difference between right and wrong? Are we sitting here waiting for a bloodbath?"

"Mister, the one on the phone, is not a psychopath." Lynn stood and strode closer to her fiancé. "Or a narcissist. He has a conscience and an understanding of right and wrong. But I don't know what emotions speaking to Lund will trigger, how incendiary the discussion may be, or the magnitude of the fallout if the conversation doesn't go the way he wants. Though what's more troubling is the fact that he's conceded he and his men may not get out of this alive."

The HTs' concern about Lund sending men after them to kill them had taken Jake by surprise. "I know you mentioned that Crispin is a pillar of the community," Jake said to Nash. "But on the phone, Mister made the guy sound like a gangster or mob boss. What does Lund do? How did he get his money?"

"Oil and gas industry," Nash said. "The Plainsman Company."

"Brian mentioned that the stolen vans were donated to a charity from an oil and gas company. What do you want to bet it's the same one?" Jake asked.

A knock came at the door.

Spinning in his chair, Aaron looked at the monitor for the security cameras. "It's Rocco."

Nash opened the door, letting the ATF agent in, and picked up his coffee.

"Forensics on the shell casings I collected on Grand Avenue came back." Rocco smiled. "My hunch panned out."

Finally. Things were coming together. Jake owed Rocco a thank-you. "Do we have confirmed IDs on two of them?"

"Unfortunately, no," Rocco said with a grimace. "There was something funny about the shell casings."

"Funny in what way?" Nash asked.

"There were two types. Live rounds and blanks."

"At least one of the gunmen is using blanks." It was a statement from Lynn, not a question. She turned to the report up on another computer screen. "Becca told you that the leader doesn't want to hurt anyone. Maybe this was how they planned to ensure no one got shot accidentally."

Jake thought back to when this kicked off and the van rolled up to the rear entrance. "A guy with a green camo mask started shooting first. I grabbed Becca and we dropped to the ground. I remembered trying to take in what kind of damage was being done. It was odd then, but everything happened too fast for me to fully process. No glass had shattered. No sound of bullets ricocheting off metal. Or hitting brick. And that's why. Because that guy was firing blanks."

Blanks shot up close could still be deadly. The fact that some of them had taken the care to use dummy rounds instead of live ones was significant.

They already knew the name of one of the gunmen who had gone into the library through the Grand Avenue entrance. Now he just needed to know if Craig Hicks was carrying blanks or live rounds.

"I take it forensics lifted prints from the blanks," Nash said, "considering the difficulty with the live rounds."

"You would be correct." Rocco's smile widened. "They belong to Troy Sims."

That meant Craig Hicks, the man who had been wearing the black paisley mask and had hit Becca, was using live ammunition. Only two gunmen had fired shots at the Grand Avenue entrance. God, how he wished that he could call her. Warn her somehow.

He whipped out his phone and fired off a quick text to her, letting her know. Surely the phone was on silent or shut off to conserve power, but she might try to contact him again and would see it then.

"Does he have a record, Troy Sims?" Jake asked as he put his phone away, wondering why they had gotten a hit off the guy's prints.

"Nope." Rocco shook his head. "Troy is a truck driver. Anyone with a commercial driver's license with HAZMAT endorsement is fingerprinted. That's how we got a match."

"HAZMAT?" Jake thought about everything they had learned, piecing it together. "Do we know where he works?"

"Yeah," Rocco said, nodding. "He's a driver for the Plainsman Oil and Gas Company."

The dots aligned, continuing to connect. Jake shot his future brother-in-law a knowing glance. Reluctantly, Nash nodded, silently relenting that this might be about more than money.

It wasn't definitive yet. The gunmen could have simply targeted a wealthy employer. A possibility they had to rule out.

Jake turned to Aaron Vance. "Dig into Crispin Lund and Plainsman Oil and Gas. Something must've happened to send those men into a tailspin that drove them to take these extreme measures. We *need* to know what it is. The sooner the better."

Aaron began clacking away on his keyboard. "I'm on it."

The contractor, Guidry, stayed suspiciously quiet and out of the way.

Jake wasn't going to look a gift horse in the mouth. "Rocco, go to Sims's place. Look around. Try to find any reason that would motivate him to invade a library and take hostages."

"Will do." But Rocco stayed planting instead of heading out. "I believe you owe me something first."

"Thank you," Jake said, with the utmost sincerity, "for taking the risk of getting your head blown off to collect the shell casings."

If the ATF agent had bothered to communicate and asked permission first, Jake would have ensured his safety while still getting the mission done. The recklessness reminded him of Becca, reviving his worry about her.

"One of our own is trapped in there," Rocco said. "I'd do it again. In a heartbeat."

Jake had no doubt that he would, as he watched him leave the mobile unit.

Outside, something stopped Rocco, causing him to hold the door open. A man and a woman, both appearing to be in their late fifties, entered. Brian was behind them.

"Mr. and Mrs. Lund, this is Supervisory Agent Nash Garner and our hostage negotiator Special Agent Jake Delgado from Denver," Brian said, making the introductions.

Jake extended his hand first to the tall, troubled-looking man with silvery strands throughout his sable hair. "Sir." They shook. He turned to his wife. Through the tears in her eyes, she forced a smile. "Mrs. Lund." He wanted to ask them to excuse his casual attire of a T-shirt and jeans, but then he realized they probably hadn't noticed what he was wearing beneath the FBI-stenciled jacket and their current emotional state.

"Detective Bradshaw has explained the situation to us," Mr. Lund said.

"I had no idea what was going on." A tear leaked from Mrs. Lund's eyes. "I don't watch television and Cameron doesn't check in with us every day."

Jake's gaze slid to Mr. Lund, who made no excuses and offered no explanations.

"Please sit down," Nash said.

The couple took seats that Lynn gestured to.

"I need to ask you some questions," Jake said, waiting a moment for the two parents to gather their thoughts. "The men inside appear to have a grievance with Mr. Lund. Sir, can you think of any reason why they would be under the impression that you've done something wrong, harmful even, that's created a debt they believe needs to be paid?"

"I don't know," Mr. Lund stammered. "Those greedy criminals will use any excuse. Violent animals. The lot of them. Probably anarchists targeting people who have struggled to get ahead and make something of themselves. It's disgraceful."

"Mr. Lund, the guy in charge in there would like to speak with you," Jake said.

"To me? About what?" His eyes widened in shock.

"To make sure I'll meet his ransom demand and he'll get his money?"

Jake took a deep breath, measuring his words. "He won't release any of the hostages until he's spoken to you personally."

Turning to her husband, Mrs. Lund looked at him expectantly. "You have to talk to him if it's the only way he'll release Cameron."

Crispin Lund shook his head as if trying to understand. "But I thought he wanted money to release Cameron."

"There are other hostages, sir," Nash said, his tone gentle. "He'll consider releasing some of them after he talks to you. There are eight other lives to take into account besides Cameron. You could help."

"Are you open to speaking with him?" Jake asked.

He hesitated, but Mrs. Lund gripped his forearm and stared at him with fresh tears welling.

"Yes, of course." Mr. Lund clasped his hands in his lap. "I'll do whatever is necessary to get our son back unharmed and to get the other hostages released."

Jake nodded. "Excuse us a moment." He pulled Brian and Nash outside and closed the door to the trailer. "Does Mr. Lund have a security team?"

"Yes," Brian said. "I had to get past them before I could speak to Mr. Lund. It was a little odd—they didn't seem surprised about the hostage situation when I informed them. I got the feeling they were aware."

"Yet, his team and Mr. Lund were sitting around at his estate twiddling their thumbs?" Nash asked.

Brian shook his head. "I got the impression, from the

whispers off to the side, not unlike what we're doing now, that they were taking some kind of action. There was a certain energy."

Precisely what the hostage takers had been worried about. "Where is his team?"

Turning, Brian pointed to three men standing by two black SUVs. "Someone is missing."

They all looked in that direction.

"Who?" Nash asked.

"His main guy," Brian said. "The creepy one who skipped the introductions. Hard-core. Ex-military. Marines."

"What was the name of the of oil and gas company that donated the two white vans, which were stolen?" Jake asked.

"The Plainsman," Brian said. "Why?"

Nash sighed. "It's Lund's company."

"So there is a connection." Brian asked.

"A big one." Jake nodded. Lund was hiding something from them. Information that could save lives. "I need you do something. One of the perps inside the library is Craig Hicks." He rattled off the man's address. "Search his place. Rocco is looking into a Troy Sims. We've got to piece this all together before it's too late."

The sheriff approached them along with a deputy.

"Russo," Sheriff Clark said, gesturing to his deputy, "was just down at Nelson's Gun and Outdoor Sports shop serving the warrant to get access to their security footage."

"How did it go?" Nash asked her. "Did they give you a hard time?"

The deputy shrugged. "Not too much. All in all, it went well. You can see the driver's full face clear as day."

"Did you send the footage over to us?" Jake asked. "We've got a techie who can run the image through a database."

"I did, but no need to waste the manpower." Deputy Russo waved her hand in a dismissive gesture.

"She recognized the driver," Sheriff Clark said.

"He used to go to my church until his sister passed away last year," Deputy Russo said. "Cancer, I believe. Then it was like he fell out with religion. Nice guy. I'm shocked he's involved in this."

"What's his name?" Jake tried to keep the spark of frustration from his voice.

"Oh, sorry." She shook her head like she was embarrassed about going off on a tangent. "Dale McKee."

"Are you sure?" Nash asked.

"One hundred percent," she said with confidence.

"McKee?" Brian scowled, his brow furrowing. "Do you know if he's any relation to a Dennis McKee."

"Yeah." Russo nodded. "They're brothers or first cousins. Either way, they're really close. Why?"

"Dennis McKee is the head of transportation for the Plainsman Oil and Gas Company," Brian said. "He oversaw the transfer of the two vans to the charity organization that the gunmen used yesterday and the security footage of the drivers who delivered them is conveniently gone."

Russo's eyebrows shot up. "No way. I can't believe Dennis is involved in this. Then again, this doesn't seem like the sort of thing Dale would do, either. He's laid-back. Unassuming. Kind of sweet."

"Dale's sister," Jake said, thinking of the woman who died from cancer. "What was her name?"

"Mary. No, that wasn't it. Marianne, I think. Why?" She looked puzzled. "What does she have to do with this?"

Jake wasn't sure. "Maybe nothing." Maybe everything. Those men were using extreme measures to take down a powerful enemy and it was obvious it must be deeply personal to one or more of them. He rubbed his hand across the stubble on his unshaved jaw, thinking. "Deputy Russo, do you know a lot of people in town?"

She gave a one-shoulder shrug. "I guess so. Grew up here. Most of the faces I see I can put a name to. Why?" she asked.

Jake took out his phone and showed her the pictures that Becca had sent to him. Brian moved in and peeked over his shoulder at the phone.

"There's Dale again." Russo pointed to the older man with the blue neck gaiter.

"What about the other one?" The leader.

"His face is familiar, but…" Russo shook her head. "Sorry. His name isn't coming to me."

"That's okay." Aaron would turn up something shortly. "We have the identities of three of the gunmen. Dale McKee. Craig Hicks. And Troy Sims. They are all connected to Plainsman. I suspect the fourth gunman, the one in charge, is, too."

"Russo," Sheriff Clark said, "we need help figuring

out who he is and why these four men are doing this. You probably know someone who can ID him."

She glanced back at the library like she was thinking. "I'll go speak to Father O'Neill down at the church. He knows everyone and everyone talks to him." She put her hands on her hips. "Might be a good place for me to start."

"What's your cell number?" Jake asked, and she gave it to him. "I'll send you the picture." Once he did, her phone chimed.

"I'll go see what I can find out about Craig Hicks," Brian said and headed out.

The mayor yelled at a deputy and then stormed past him, stalking toward them.

"I'll handle him." The sheriff tipped his hat and left to intercept Schroeder.

Jake was grateful he didn't have to deal with the man. There was a more pressing issue that required his attention. He and Nash went back inside the trailer.

"Mr. Lund," Jake said, "are you ready for us to make this call?"

"Yes." He pulled on a brave face as his wife clutched his arm. "I'm ready."

Jake picked up the phone and dialed the number, putting the call on speaker.

Mister answered on the first ring. "Jake, is that you?"

"It is."

"Do you have him there?"

"Yes," Jake said. "Mr. Lund is here and is willing to speak with you." Jake gestured for him to go ahead.

"Hello. This is Crispin Lund."

"I won't waste my breath or time explaining how much I hate you or why," Mister said. "Because you already know."

"What?" Confusion was written across Lund's face. "I don't even know who you are. How could I possibly understand your misplaced hatred?"

"You don't know my name because you thought I had no more importance than a fly in your coffee. You dismissed me and the others, with pennies from your pocket. Not anymore. In addition to the six and half million dollars, we want the evidence you buried. Turn it over to the FBI. And…we want a public apology."

Nash hit the mute button. "What is he talking about?"

Throwing his hands up, Lund shrugged. "I have no idea."

"The part about a payoff should jog your memory," Jake said, "if buried evidence doesn't."

"Look here, I'm a businessman." Mr. Lund straightened in his seat. "Once a week I solve problems by writing a check. That nobody could be talking about a hundred different things."

It was a lie, and a bad one. "Then that's a lot of buried evidence," Jake said.

Nash threw him a harsh glare of warning.

"If you dismiss that man again," Lynn said, "by saying that you don't know what he's talking about, it's likely to trigger him."

Lund sighed. "But I don't know. What do you expect me to do? Make up something to appease his delusions. Listen, I'm willing to pay the ransom demand. Nothing is more important than the life of our son. Agent Delgado, you need to do your job. Negotiate."

Not willing to keep the call on hold any longer, Jake unmuted the phone. "You've spoken to Mr. Lund and made your demands clear. How about you release some hostages?"

"First, I want Lund to say that he'll do it. Hand over the evidence and apologize."

"Sure, whatever you want. Just don't hurt Cameron," Mr. Lund said, and his wife nudged him. "Or anyone else."

"Liar!"

At the roar on the other end of the line, Mr. Lund reeled back in his chair, startled. Mrs. Lund clutched her throat, jaw unhinged, looking horrified.

"Mr. Lund just agreed." Jake kept his tone calm, his focus razor-sharp. "Why do you think he's lying?"

"Whenever the devil opens his mouth, he lies. This isn't any different."

"This is nonsense," Mr. Lund whispered. "I have no reason to lie and every reason to protect Cameron."

Jake hoped that was true. "I think we should give him the benefit of the doubt. A chance to follow through."

"Well, that's a problem. You fool me once, shame on you. Fool me twice, shame on me. I already know I'm dealing with a despicable man who can't be trusted."

Momentum was everything. Not letting the process stall was crucial. "There must be some way that he can prove his sincerity. Why don't we start with the payment of the ransom."

Mister sighed. "He can prove himself right now. If he's

telling the truth and intends to hand over the evidence, I want to hear *him* tell *you* what this is really about."

Everyone in the trailer stared at Mr. Lund. His wife's brow furrowed in confusion, or perhaps it was doubt.

Shaking his head, Lund resolutely looked anywhere but at his wife, maintaining a perplexed expression. "I swear," he whispered, "I don't know what he's talking about."

Either lying came as easily as breathing to Crispin Lund or he was giving an Oscar-worthy performance.

Aaron snapped his fingers, catching Jake's attention. He hurried down to where his techie was sitting and looked over his shoulder at the screen.

There was a picture of the guy with the blue neck gaiter. Identity confirmed as Dale McKee. Beside it was the photo of Mister. Along with a name. Frank Ferguson. An address. Also, the name of his deceased wife, who died last year. Marianne McKee-Ferguson.

Nodding thanks to Aaron, Jake scooted back over to the phone.

"I'm waiting," Frank, said. "Why isn't he telling you?"

"I don't know what madness has driven you to do this," Mr. Lund said into the speaker. "But I will gladly pay the ransom money for you to stop." His tone was desperate in his plea to placate the man holding his son and others hostage. "I can have the money ready in the morning."

"Give us the account number." Jake was hoping to redirect. Focus the discussion on one concrete thing that was possible. "As soon as the money is ready, it'll be wired."

Frank gave the account number. "It's offshore and untraceable."

"I'll see what I can do to expedite the transfer," Lund offered.

Nodding, Jake thought that was a good touch. The faster the better.

But Frank groaned. "Of course, you're willing to pay a few million now that we have your son," he said, sounding as if he was speaking through gritted teeth. "You should've done that when we came to you last year, before people started dying, Lund. Now we want more. We want everything! Tell the FBI what this is about, and we'll release more hostages. We'll start with Tyler Schroeder and the pregnant lady."

Jake's chest tightened at the thought of Becca's release being dependent on Mr. Lund's actions.

Facing a similar concern, Guidry hopped up, skirted past everyone and bolted out of the trailer. No doubt running to the mayor, who would in turn attempt to coerce Mr. Lund.

"If you don't," Frank said, "you refuse to produce the evidence and give us a public apology, we will send your son back to you in pieces. Do you hear me? Pieces!"

"Oh, God," Mrs. Lund cried out through a sob, collapsing in on herself. "Crispin, what have you done? What have you gotten our boy mixed up in?"

Mr. Lund stiffened, turning stoic, saying nothing. He didn't even attempt to look at his wife, let alone comfort her.

His sister approached Mrs. Lund and patted her back as she whispered to the distraught woman.

"Frank," Jake said, clenching his hand at his side. "I don't think you're a murderer. You, Dale, Craig and Troy don't want to kill anybody." Although that might not apply to all of them, since at least one was using live ammunition.

"Finally figured out who we are, huh?"

"Yes, we have," Jake said. It was always a matter of time.

"Changes nothing. My wife is dead. Because of Lund. Craig is divorced. I made sure the men I picked to take the library with me don't have any family at home for Lund's people to threaten. Nothing to lose."

Mrs. Lund wept harder despite Lynn's efforts to calm her.

"Killing Cameron, someone blameless in this, isn't the answer," Jake said, over Mrs. Lund's sobs. "Murder could get you life imprisonment. It isn't worth it."

"First of all, you're talking to a dead man walking. A life sentence means nothing. Second, who said anything about killing?" Frank asked. "His son can lose fingers, toes and other body parts that would be nice to have, but not essential to live."

Mrs. Lund wailed while her husband sat stone-faced. "Don't," she said, sobbing. "How can you be such a monster?"

"I'm not the monster here. Your son will live. While my sweet Marianne is dead. I had to watch her wither away, slowly, painfully. Because of your husband. He's the real monster."

Mrs. Lund stared at her husband with tears streaming down her anguished face.

"Listen to me, Frank." Jake could feel this spiraling out of his hands and needed to regain control. "Don't take any irrevocable steps. Some things once done, can't be undone."

Frank sighed. "That's the whole point."

"Please," Mrs. Lund pleaded into the speaker. "Please don't hurt my son!"

"You're begging the wrong person," Frank said. "Your husband can stop this any time he sees fit. His choice whether Cameron gets hurt. In two hours, noon, he stands in front of the press gathered outside and tells them what he did to us. Then he will issue an apology and hand Agent Jake Delgado the evidence he buried. Jake will verify the contents on live television. If this doesn't happen, you all know the consequences. I'll start with your boy's finger, Crispin. The ball is in your court."

Chapter Ten

Tugging gloves onto his hands, Brian didn't think that his search would take long. Craig Hicks's house was small. One story. Less than a thousand square feet.

It was located on the far outskirts of town, off the Snowy Range Road, closer to Centennial and the Plainsman oil rigs than downtown.

Blinds covered the windows, blocking out the sunlight and leaving the house dimly lit. Brian entered the only bedroom near the door. The room was untidy, the bed not made, a light layer of dust on the dresser.

He opened a drawer. The usual. Underwear. Socks. Clothes in the others.

On top of the single nightstand were two empty beer bottles. Inside the drawer, there wasn't much, either. Nothing of note.

Next, he checked the single bathroom in the place. A pedestal sink, a dirty toilet and a soap-scum covered shower the size of a phone booth were crammed into the space. He opened the medicine cabinet. On the bottom shelf were a few hygiene and grooming products. Prescription bottles packed the top shelf. Taking out his cell phone, he snapped some photos of the labels. With the exception of the painkillers, the rest of the medicines he didn't recognize and couldn't tell what they were for.

Exiting the bathroom, he moved to the living area. A shabby pleather couch faced an entertainment center. The TV was an older-model, thirty-two-inch flat screen. A game console and controller sat beside it.

He headed for the kitchen, a narrow clutter of unwashed dishes and empty beer bottles. Housekeeping clearly wasn't a priority for Craig. A stack of papers on the counter in between the fridge and sink caught his eye. He thumbed through them. All bills. All past due. The mortgage. Utilities. Then he understood why. Beneath those was a mountain of medical bills. Cardiac problems and cancer.

From the looks of it, Craig Hicks was not only sick. He was dying.

ONE HOUR BLED into another and another as the temperature in the library steadily climbed. The hands on the clock crept closer to high noon. Soon the heat would be unbearable. If only the gunmen would open a window and the door to the story time room for some fresh air. It was stifling in there.

Resting her head back against the wall, Becca could barely breathe. Beads of sweat rolled down her temple. Her hands were clammy. Her throat was dry. She opened her bottle of water and poured the last few drops into her mouth, praying they would get more soon.

"You don't look well, dear," Abigail said.

"I'm fine." She would be. That was what she kept telling herself. "Just hot. And thirsty."

The older woman smiled at her. "Hopefully, they'll give us more water soon."

Food, too, she prayed. Although Becca's morning sickness hadn't passed, a bag of pretzels would do her some good. Get her blood sugar up. Clear the fog of hunger clogging her mind, dampening her thoughts.

But this suffocating heat was draining. Weakening her willpower to fight.

Don't give in.

She needed to stay sharp, ready to act if she had a chance.

Movement registered beyond the glass window of the room.

"Here they come now," Abigail said, perking up. "Maybe it's to give us food and water."

Becca doubted it.

Holding their weapons instead of nourishment, Gray and Camo were stalking to the story time room. Their neck gaiters were down, revealing their full faces.

Angry faces.

Not a good sign.

Why were they no longer concerned with hiding their identities? Had Jake figured out who they were? Had the pictures helped?

Keys jangled outside the room as Gray unlocked and opened the door. Both men strode inside.

"Why are you showing us your faces?" Nolan asked, alarm in his voice as his eyes widened. "Oh, God. Are you going to kill us? Is that why?"

Tyler brought his knees up into his chest like he wanted to make himself as small as possible. Becca put a comforting arm around him. She wanted to tell the boy that it would be okay, but it felt like a hollow platitude as she stared at those two men who were livid over something.

"We don't intend to kill anyone," Gray said. "There's no longer a need to hide our faces because the FBI knows who we are."

Yes. A step in the right direction. It was all Becca could do not to fist-pump the air. "Can we know your names?" She was tired of referring to them by the color of their masks.

"I'm Frank," he said, his tone clipped, his expression severe. "It's up to him if he wants to tell you his name." He hiked his chin at his cohort.

With a grunt, the other guy shook his head, not interested in sharing.

"Cameron," Frank said, "it doesn't look like your father is going to cooperate."

"What?" The young millennial sat upright. "Cooperate with what? Giving you money?"

"Giving us what he owes us. In addition to doing the right thing," Frank clarified. "That's unfortunate for you."

"For me?" Cringing in fear, Cameron looked around the room at everyone. "Why?"

Dread ran cold through Becca. What were they going to do to him?

Frank gestured to the bigger guy, who withdrew a syringe from the pocket of his cargo pants and prowled toward Cameron.

"What's in that?" The librarian tried to scoot back to get away, but the wall stopped his retreat. There was nowhere for him to go.

"Whatever you're planning," Becca said, climbing to her feet, "you don't have to do it." A wave of dizziness engulfed her. She swayed, darkness edging in around the periphery of her vision. Reaching out, she put a hand on the wall to steady herself.

"I'm warning you." Frank pointed at her. "Stay out of this. What happens to him is his father's fault. Not ours." He nodded at the big guy, giving him the go-ahead.

"No, please," Cameron begged, cowering.

"Are you right- or left-handed?" the man with the green camo neck gaiter asked, his tone hard and cold as ice.

Trembling, Cameron started to hyperventilate. "Right."

The big guy snatched the Cameron's left hand.

"What are you going to do him?" Becca demanded, unable to stay silent.

"Chop off one of his fingers," Frank said. "We'll start with the pinkie."

Gasps resounded around the room. Cameron looked as if he might pass out as tears leaked from his eyes.

Start? Were they planning to take more from him?

Using his mouth, the big man pulled the cap off the syringe.

"W-w-what's that?" Cameron asked.

Frank stepped deeper into the room. "Something to numb the area, so you're not in too much pain. We want your father to suffer. Not you."

Becca's gaze fell to the gun in Frank's hand, flew

to the one holstered on the big guy's hip, and bounced to the glass window. Frank was standing close to her, where she could disarm him, possibly fast enough to turn the gun on the big guy before he withdrew his Glock. But she had no idea how long it would take Craig to show up and that man would not hesitate to put a bullet in her or one of the other hostages.

She had to do something.

"He'll die." The desperate words flew from her mouth. Anything to give them pause. To stop them. "He'll bleed out." There were no large veins or arteries in his fingers. If sufficient pressure was applied, the wound would clot. Slim chance of him bleeding out, but she was desperate enough to say anything.

Frank pulled something from his cargo pocket. A mini blowtorch. The butane kind that someone would use for cooking. "We'll cauterize it."

Nolan and Cameron both looked like they were going to be sick.

The hostage takers had planned for something this gruesome. This awful. From the very beginning.

As the big guy looked at the librarian's hand, drawing the tip of the needle closer, Becca's mind whirled, strategizing a way to avoid this, but she couldn't think of any.

If she couldn't prevent it, then she needed to do triage. "Wait!" She held up a palm but didn't dare step closer. "Not the pinkie."

"Why not?" Frank asked.

Losing a pinkie meant losing 50 percent of the strength in your hand, was the first thought to fly into her head, but not the last. "He plays the piano. Every day. Loves it. He needs all his fingers. Don't take that from him because of whatever his father did."

Frank mulled it over a moment. "Fine. Then a toe."

The lackey with the muscles dropped Cameron's hand and grabbed his ankle, drawing it up into the air. Sticking the syringe between his teeth, he yanked off the man's shoe and sock. Nolan gagged before turning his face toward the wall. Tyler lowered his forehead to his knees that he had brought up to his chest.

Triage. Do what you can. "Not the little or big toe," she said.

The brute stared at her, his eyes narrowing, before looking to Frank. The boss nodded. Then the guy stuck the needle near the base of the one next to the little toe. Cameron hissed in pain as the contents were injected from the syringe.

"We'll give it twenty minutes to kick in," Frank said. "Then we'll be back to take it." They turned to leave.

Whimpering, Cameron curled up in a fetal position.

She couldn't imagine what he was thinking or feeling. How terrified he must be, anticipating, dreading what was to come. All she knew was that she had to do more to help him. "Wait, please. I, um, I need to use the bathroom."

If she could call Jake with the last of the power left in the phone, explain what was happening, the severity, the brutal turn the situation was about to take, maybe he could do something.

He was the miracle worker after all.

"You'll have to wait," Frank said.

Becca put a hand to her stomach. "It can't wait."

"She still has morning sickness." Abigail climbed to her feet and cupped her arm for support. "The heat and lack of water has made it worse. Can you find it in your hearts to let her use the facilities? I'll go with her to make sure she's okay in there."

Frank sighed. "Take them," he said.

Grunting, the other man gave a tight nod. "All right." He beckoned to them with a large hand. "Come on."

Becca wasn't feeling her best with the lingering dizziness, low blood sugar and what she suspected was low blood pressure as well. Still, she could've made it to the restroom on her own, but she thought it best to pretend to need Abigail's assistance, leaning on the older woman, as they walked to the bathroom.

If she could only splash some cold water on her face, hydrate and eat, she'd regain her full strength.

They pushed through the bathroom door. Once it closed shut, she listened for a second as the big fellow shuffled off to the side.

There wasn't much time.

Tension pulsed through Becca as she bent over and grabbed the phone from her boot. She pressed the power button and held it until the cell phone lit up.

Abigail's eyes grew wide. "You hid a phone?"

"I took it from Paige Pietsch." Staring at the screen as it cycled through bringing up apps, she willed the phone to power up faster.

"But they warned us." Abigail's voice grew low. "The consequences—"

"I had to," she said, cutting her off.

"It's too dangerous." The strangest expression fell across Abigail's face. "Why risk it?"

Was the poor woman afraid that she would be caught, and everyone would suffer the consequences?

Grimacing, Becca didn't have precious minutes to squander explaining it fully. "I've been in contact with the FBI," she said. A text popped up. Ignoring it, she accessed the recent calls list.

"I don't understand." Abigail shook her head, her face tightening with confusion and concern. "How?"

She tapped Jake's number. "I'm an FBI agent." Then she hit the call icon. "I've been talking to the lead negotiator. I know him." Personally. Intimately. But she left that out.

The line rang.

Abigail stared at her, alarm glistening in her eyes and slapped the phone out of her hand.

The cell clattered to the tile floor.

"What are you thinking?" Becca snapped, trying to keep her voice down.

"She's got a phone!" Abigail turned and ran for the door.

"What are you doing?" Trying to shush her, Becca went after the older woman. "Be quiet. I'm trying to help us."

"Troy! Hurry!"

Becca's heartbeat drummed in her ears. Her body pumped a fresh load of adrenaline into her bloodstream. Grim reality set in as a million things tumbled through her mind in nanoseconds. Abigail had just betrayed her. The older woman knew this hostage taker's name. Because Abigail was one of them. An inside person—a spy—who'd been watching the hostages, gaining their trust, making sure they stayed in line, this entire time.

"Hello." Jake's voice came from the phone on the floor.

The big guy barreled into the bathroom.

"She's an FBI agent," Abigail said, venom in her tone, her demeanor hardening. "She's calling that negotiator. They're friends."

Troy rushed Becca.

The man was big. Six-three. Two hundred pounds of solid muscle. But he was also slow and didn't move like a skilled fighter.

Becca threw a kick with the solid stacked heel of her boot, hitting his kneecap squarely, shattering it. Troy bellowed and sagged, somehow staying on his feet.

She grabbed the barrel of the gun, twisting his wrist in a manner that would leave it sprained. With a fist, she punched the inside of his wrist, knocking the gun from his hand. The weapon went skidding across the tile.

Abigail tore out of the bathroom. The door closed behind her, but her voice carried. "Frank! Craig!"

Becca had to keep moving. Troy wasn't down yet. She rammed the heel of her palm up into his nose. Bone crunched. The palm strike sent the big guy staggering backward on his one good leg as he howled louder in agonizing pain. While his head was tipped back, she jabbed at his throat. Her fist struck his windpipe.

Troy made a choking sound, smothering his cries. Coughing and gagging, he bent over, clutching his throat. Just like she had expected.

"Becca! Are you all right? Becca!" Jake yelled from the phone on the floor, his voice low, sounding far away.

She slammed Troy's head down against one of the sinks as hard as she could.

The man slumped to the floor in a heap, rendered unconscious.

Chest heaving from the exertion, she knelt and tapped the speaker button on the phone but didn't bother to pick it up since she still needed to use both hands. She scanned the floor. Found the gun near a stall. She grabbed it. "Jake, I'm burned." She hustled over to Troy, checked his cargo pocket and found zip ties. "I'm in trouble."

"What happened?" Jake's voice was tight with concern. "What's going on?"

She restrained Troy with his hands behind his back, using the plastic zip ties. "They're preparing to mutilate Cameron. They're serious. You have to stop it. I've taken the big guy down, but—"

The bathroom door burst open.

Becca pivoted, taking aim at whoever stood in the doorway. Craig. She had the gun pointed at him, center mass. All she had to do was pull the trigger. "FBI. Do not take another step."

Craig's gaze dipped to unconscious Troy and bounced back to her. A sinister smile stretched across his mouth. "Or what?"

Steadying her grip on the weapon with her sweaty palms, she stood and said, "Or I will shoot."

"Oh, God, Becca." Jake's grim voice over the speaker, echoed in the room.

"Then shoot." Craig stalked inside the bathroom, closing the distance between them, a Glock in his hand.

She leveled the weapon, slid her finger to the trigger, ready to fire. "I'm warning you."

"Most of the men are using blanks," Jake said.

A cold dread gripped her belly like a fist.

Craig's evil grin spread to his eyes as he prowled closer.

She pulled the trigger in rapid succession. *Pop, pop, pop.*

No spots of blood bloomed on his chest. Standing unharmed, Craig chuckled. "Everyone has blanks." He pointed his Glock at her head. "Except for me." He cocked the gun.

The metallic clacking sent a bolt of fear straight to her heart.

She dropped the firearm. Then she raised her hands slowly.

Craig lowered the muzzle. He shot the phone twice, shattering it into pieces. Redirecting the aim, he pointed the weapon back at her. "Get down on the floor. Face-down. And put your hands behind your back."

He wasn't within arm's reach to even attempt to disarm him. The gun was pointed at her head. If he fired, that would be it. She would be dead.

Left with no choice, she did what he told her to, lying down on the floor, her cheek pressing to the cold tile.

"All women need to learn their place. But some feisty ones like you need harder lessons than others." He put a knee against her back, on her spine, his weight squeezing the air from her lungs as he restrained her with a zip tie.

Becca was in so far over her head, there was no way she could reach the surface before she drowned.

Not alone, anyway.

Come on, Jake.

I need a miracle.

Chapter Eleven

Frustration tangled with fear, burning Jake's gut.

Multiple shots had been fired inside the library. The line with Becca disconnected. He hadn't been able to hear much of anything before she put the call on speaker. Maybe noises as though there was a fight. After that, it had sounded like a showdown between her and Craig. She had been at such a huge disadvantage not knowing most of the guns probably had blanks.

Now Jake didn't know if Becca was injured. Or even alive.

Please be alive.

They knew she was an FBI agent. Everything was about to change. Calling Frank now, unprepared and on the verge of being unhinged, with nothing to offer him would be a grave mistake that could make Becca's situation worse.

Jake gritted his teeth. "I've got to get in there." He needed to know what was happening and assess the situation. Get a visual on Becca. Get anyone who required it medical attention.

"Hold on." Nash raked a hand through his hair. "Things

have just gone to hell in a handbasket in that library. We have no idea why things have escalated inside, and you want to do what exactly? Storm in there, guns blazing?"

"No." Of course, not. "But I need a way in." He stared at the various angles of the library on the monitors in the command center. Trying to sneak in could prove catastrophic, complicating things further. Some degree of trust was just lost with Frank. He had to earn it back while checking on Becca at the same time. "A way for Frank to let me in. I've got to see if Becca is all right."

"Don't go off the rails on me," Nash said. "Not now. I need you calm and focused more than ever. Not a loose cannon."

No matter what, Jake was never a loose cannon. He didn't unravel under pressure. Although he was close to his breaking point, he had yet to reach it.

Grabbing a cold bottle of water, he pushed past Nash and headed for the door.

"Where are you going?" Nash asked, right behind him.

"To get fresh air and some answers." He flung the door of the trailer open. "We need to know what Lund is hiding."

Crispin had remained unflappable, sticking to his denial that there was any culpability on his part. Even after Frank had threatened to send him his son in pieces. And his wife had begged him to cooperate, to sacrifice, to do whatever was necessary to spare their boy.

Jake came up with one conclusion.

The CEO of Plainsman Oil and Gas had a lot to lose, more than six and a half million dollars. Frank had said that they wanted everything. The evidence that Frank was demanding was at the core of it. But Lund wasn't about to give up the proof for anything—not even for Cameron.

It disgusted and horrified Jake. Revulsion welled in the back of his throat, a sour taste that lingered. His hand clenched into a fist unconsciously, and he had to force himself to uncurl it. There was a special place in hell for men like Lund.

Jake jumped down the stairs of the trailer and scanned the area. His gaze swept past the sheriff, who was talking to reporters, as Jake looked for the callous, self-centered man who would do anything to protect himself.

There!

Lund was face-to-face with Schroeder in a heated argument. Mrs. Lund, off to the side, appeared inconsolable despite his sister's best professional efforts.

"How dare you threaten me!" Lund shouted, drawing the attention of his security team. "Who do you think you are?"

"The mayor. A father. A gun-carrying citizen who is not afraid to use his weapon."

"Are you implying that you'll shoot me?"

The three men from Lund's security team gathered around him, reminding Jake that there was a fourth man unaccounted for, out there somewhere.

Schroeder put his hands on his hips. "If that's what it'll take, those gunmen seeing your dead body, to get my son released, then yeah, I'm considering it."

"I'm handling this on multiple levels," Lund said. "You'd do best to stay out of my way."

"Handling it how?" the mayor demanded. "On what levels? Fill me in or I'll throw so many wrenches into your wheelhouse that it will make your head spin."

Sighing, Nash started to go intervene, but Jake held him back.

"What are you doing?" his future brother-in-law asked. "I need to separate those two."

Jake shook his head. "That's the last thing you need to do. This is why Frank won't let Tyler Schroeder go."

"What do you mean?"

"Look at them. Two sharks going at each other," Jake said, finally realizing. "The mayor is the only one who can put enough pressure on Lund to do the right thing." Not even Mrs. Lund's grief moved that cold-blooded man. "And Schroeder is highly motivated since his son is captive in the library." More pieces started to come together for him. "The devil is a liar."

"That's what Frank called Lund."

Jake nodded. "I don't think Frank ever expected Crispin Lund to follow through on his own accord. He was hoping that sending him Cameron in pieces might persuade him if the mayor failed to."

"Where does that leave us?"

At an impasse. Lund was calling the hostage-taker's bluff. Jake had no doubt that Frank would follow through.

"In need of the truth," Jake said, "about what really happened to incite this."

The hostility between Lund and Schroeder had cooled down from a rapid boil to a simmer. Lund was saying something to Schroeder in a low voice that had the mayor leaning in.

What were they plotting? What deal with the devil was being struck?

The anger inside Jake was molten, bubbling, rising to the surface of his skin. He opened his bottle of water and chugged it. Cool liquid slid down his throat, but it did nothing to chill the hot swirl of emotions in his belly.

Stay in control. Stay strong.

Entering the restricted area for cleared personnel only was Deputy Russo. She was walking with a man dressed in black, wearing a clerical collar. A priest.

"Agent Garner, Agent Delgado, this is Father O'Neill," Deputy Russo said, and they shook hands. "He identified the fourth man as Frank Ferguson. He was married to Dale's sister, Marianne."

"We've figured that out," Jake said. "I hope you didn't bring the father over for just that. We'd hate to waste your time, sir."

"No. There's more. Can we speak inside, away from prying eyes?" Russo asked.

Lund had stopped talking. He and Schroeder were staring at them.

"Right this way," Jake said, gesturing to the command center. They all climbed into the mobile unit. "Please have a seat."

The priest sank into a chair.

"Father, please tell them what you told me," Deputy Russo said, choosing to remain standing. "I thought it best for you to hear it directly from him."

"I'll share what I told the deputy, but you must understand I will not divulge the names of any of my parishioners. They confide in me. That trust is sacred. Considering the current circumstances, I believe some leeway would be permissible."

"We don't need to know who told you," Jake said. "But we need to know what they shared, if it can shed any light on the gunmen's motives."

"A lot of folks depend on the Plainsman Oil and Gas Company for their livelihoods. Some also live out near the rigs. About two years ago, while they were doing some hydrofracking, there was a horrible accident," Father O'Neill said. "Deadly chemicals were released. Crispin Lund made sure the story about the accident never saw the light of day. He has powerful friends in high places. Not just locally. I have it on good authority that he's contributed heavily to the campaigns of certain senators, one being the ranking member of the committee on energy and natural resources. He's also very tight with Tom Teller."

"The owner of one of the biggest multinational news networks?" Nash asked.

O'Neill nodded. "The one and the same."

That was why Frank was paranoid about being silenced. Lund had done it once before. There was nothing stopping him from doing it again. Unless every major news station was covering the story.

"Shortly after the accident," the priest said, "people started getting sick. They went to Crispin in the hopes that he would make it right. He blew them off. At first. The workers involved in the accident and some who lived in the surrounding area of where it happened decided to pursue a class action lawsuit. They found someone on the board willing to give them evidence. Then the woman turned up dead. The evidence buried."

Lund would stoop so low as to have someone murdered.

Was there no line he wouldn't cross to protect his interests?

Father O'Neill crossed his legs and clasped his hands. "Next, Lund's people went around offering the would-be claimants fifteen thousand dollars each in exchange for signing a nondisclosure agreement. With mounting bills and medical expenses, most of them were desperate for whatever they could get and signed. Their fancy lawyer told the holdouts that they needed a couple of dozen people for a successful class action lawsuit. Not onesie-twosies. But more importantly they also needed the evidence. Sounds obvious that their illnesses were related to the company's fracking, but they needed more legal ammunition than 'it just makes sense.' A number of those individuals have since died from various health conditions."

"Such as?" Jake asked.

"They run the gamut. Respiratory. Endocrine. Gastrointestinal. Cardiac. Cancer. The ones who haven't died are terribly sick. They're living on borrowed time. It's a tragedy. One that persists each day Lund refuses to make it right."

That explained the ton of meds and piles of debts Brian and Rocco had found at the homes of Craig Hicks and Troy Sims.

"What about the death of the board member?" Nash asked. "Who investigated it?"

"The old sheriff."

"Jim Ames." Nash groaned. "He turned out to be as corrupt as could be. No doubt paid off. If Daniel knew about it, he would look into it. Reopen the case."

"Are you sure the new sheriff wouldn't be more concerned with getting a campaign contribution from Lund?" Jake asked.

Nash frowned at him. "Positive. Daniel Clark won't let sleeping dogs lie. Not when it comes to murder. He'll pursue justice even if it means he doesn't win the election."

"Good to hear that," the father said. "If Sheriff Clark did reopen the case, it would go a long way in earning him support. If he solved it, put someone behind bars for the murder, I think he'd win by a landslide."

"Father O'Neill," Jake said, wanting to steer the clergyman back to the hostage situation, "I don't think that these men just want money. They're looking for justice, aren't they?"

"Though their methods are wrong, I believe so. Not that I can say for certain." Father O'Neill stood. "I hope that was useful, but I don't think I can be of any more assistance."

"There is one more thing, Father." Jake scrubbed a hand across his jaw, thinking. "Do you have any idea why Frank and the others have chosen to act now?"

"I'm not sure I know what you mean. I suppose they were desperate and at their wits' end."

"It's been two years since the accident," Jake said.

"One since their efforts to sue failed. Any idea why now? Why yesterday?"

Father O'Neill mulled it over a moment. "The only thing I can come up with is that the anniversary of Marianne's death was this month. Beyond that I couldn't say."

"Okay. Thank you, Father." Jake shook his hand.

"We appreciate your time, and thanks for the thorough follow-up, Deputy Russo." Nash showed them out. "Thoughts?" he asked Jake.

"I think I know a way to convince Frank to let me inside the building." He could check on Becca and the others.

"That's not the only urgent goal." Nash leaned against the back wall and folded his arms. "See what you can do to make sure Cameron Lund doesn't lose any body parts. That kid shouldn't have to pay for his father's sins."

Jake couldn't agree more. There was less than ten minutes until the deadline. He dialed the line to the library and put it on speaker. As it began to ring, his heart kicked in his chest like an angry horse.

He met Nash's steady gaze. His almost brother-in-law nodded in encouragement as the phone rang and rang.

Wasn't Frank going to pick up? God, what if he didn't?

Sweat beaded along the edge of his forehead. He wiped it away, trying to breathe through the nerves.

Should he hang up? Try again? Grab another bullhorn and go out there.

It had been ringing too long.

There was a click.

His heart leaped and dropped as silence stretched out.

Then finally, "You've been playing me for a fool, Jake."

Hope bolted through him, followed immediately by dread at the striking anger in Frank's tone.

Jake could almost picture him there, standing at the information desk, sweating in the mounting heat, listening to the choppers overhead, trying to gather the presence of mind to do…what? Hurt Cameron? Use Becca if she was still alive?

He needed to end this. Fury coupled with kamikaze bravado was a recipe for disaster.

"I haven't, Frank. I want this resolved peacefully. With everyone alive."

"You're a liar just like Lund. Noticed you didn't say anything about the pregnant lady being your FBI friend."

"Is she alive?" Jake asked.

"Yeah, she's breathing."

Thank God. Relief flared in Jake's chest. "Have you hurt her?" Heaven help them if they had.

"She's the one who's been hurting others," Frank said, and that sounded like Becca. "But that's about to change in five minutes when we take Cameron's first appendage."

Jake drew in a deep breath. "Maiming Cameron will get you nothing."

"We'll see about that. Lund thinks he can stomach anything. Wait until he sees his boy's toe in a box."

Squeezing his eyes shut at the gruesome imagery, Jake refocused. "I know that Lund is a corrupt, cold-hearted scumbag. He's willing to let you mutilate his son in order to keep his secrets. I understand how he wronged you. Marianne. And the others. But hurting Cameron will change nothing. Besides making you the bad guys in the eyes of everyone else. Don't become a villain trying to take one down."

"He has left us with no other choice."

"Don't give him any more power over you by letting him take away your options. Frank, I have an alternative for you. I can't let reporters in to interview you the way that you want. But I can give you a chance to tell your story. The way you want."

"How?"

"Let me in with my phone. I'll let you stream whatever statement you want to make live on YouTube and—"

"No! No, YouTube. Me posting some video isn't credible. I want to be on every major network. Prime time."

"And you will. You didn't let me finish. We will notify the media that you'll be interviewed by me. They will all tune in to the FBI's official channel and record it as we stream live. Simultaneously."

Nash met his gaze and nodded, then he moved down and spoke quietly to Aaron.

Jake hoped they were smoothing the way to make it happen in the event Frank agreed. "Every major news outlet will replay the video multiple times, including during prime time. It doesn't get any bigger or more legitimate than that," he said. "I can make sure the world hears you. Lay it all out for them. About the accident. The murder of a board member who tried to help you. How the previous sheriff who was corrupt turned a blind eye. The NDAs. Everything you know or suspect about Lund's powerful friends. Name them. You get to say it all. A story that juicy will have the full power of the press focused on digging to uncover the truth. Trust me, there'll be at least one dogged reporter who will find specifics. I can also assure you that the new sheriff will look into reopening the cold case on the Plainsman Oil and Gas board member who was killed."

"Jennifer Paulson."

"If Crispin Lund is guilty, the press won't just find out. They will destroy him. Let's get your story out there. What do you say?"

There was silence. A long, nerve-wracking pause. In that desperate moment, Jake hoped that he had hooked him.

Please let him take the bait and be satisfied.

"That's not good enough," Frank said.

Jake's hope crumbled. He wanted to smash his fist into something, but instead he listened.

"Devils like Lund somehow wriggle free," Frank said. "He won't stay down for long. He'll rise out of this like a phoenix from the ashes. Unless we get cold, hard evidence. But…getting our story out there, on every network, unleashing the vultures to pick at him, is a good place to start. A necessary one. I want someone to announce that I'll be speaking, so they can all expect it."

Releasing the breath that he had been holding, Jake unclenched his hand. "In exchange, you agree not to hurt Cameron and to release Tyler, Abigail and Special Agent Becca Hammond."

"Cameron will get to keep his fingers and toes until six p.m. The interview will buy him a few more hours. But you had better make Crispin Lund understand that there is a price to be paid and I mean more than money. You can have Abigail. Your FBI agent, the schoolteacher and Tyler stay until the six and a half million hits the account. Then they'll be released along with four more."

"I need the last minor."

"I think I'll hang on to him."

Sighing, Jake decided to try a different angle. "Tyler is of no use to you. Mayor Schroeder hasn't been able to coerce Lund to cooperate further. Despite his best efforts. You have to release Tyler, too." Pushing for Becca and Russell Nolan might have been a bridge to far to cross. But he had to try to get the kid out. "When we livestream wouldn't you like to be able to say that you let *all* the kids go? Help paint the picture that you're not the bad guys."

Frank didn't say anything. Jake thought he might have to nudge him harder on this.

But then he said, "Okay. You can have Tyler, also."

A win he would have to take for now. It gave them more time as well as the freedom of Tyler and Abigail.

"I'll need to see Becca to verify that she's all right and hasn't been hurt."

"Agreed. Get things set up. Once it's ready, let me know," Frank added. "We'll open the same window on Seventh. Abigail and Tyler will come out. Then you'll climb through. If you come in armed or try any funny business, there'll be hell to pay."

Chapter Twelve

With her hands bound behind her back and duct tape over her mouth, Becca sat in a corner on the opposite side of the room from Abigail.

"I had to do it." Tears streamed down the charlatan's face. "She was going to get all of us in trouble," the older woman said. "I had to tell them she had a phone. To spare the rest of us whatever consequences she's going to bring down on her own head. Do you think I did the right thing? Trying to protect us?"

The woman was full of tricks. A master at manipulation.

"Of course, you did." Russell Nolan's tone was sympathetic. Then he glared at Becca like she was the fiend. "She obviously didn't care if the rest of us were going to get punished. If she wants to be denied food and water, that is on her. We should not have to suffer alongside her."

"I was just so scared." Abigail trembled. "They said there would be consequences if they found a phone."

"What if she was trying to help somehow?" Cameron asked.

Thank you.

"Help how?" Abigail snapped. "The FBI is already

out there negotiating for our release. All we have to do is keep our heads down. Cooperate."

"Speak for yourself." Cameron looked down at his foot. "They're not about to cut off your toe."

Tyler shivered and put his head back down on his knees.

"What were you thinking?" Frank shouted out near the information desk. "Carrying live ammunition!"

"I was thinking better safe than sorry," Craig bellowed back.

They were fighting among themselves. That was good. A weakened bond Jake could exploit.

"You could've killed someone by accident, you fool." Outrage poured through Frank's tone.

"I'm not the fool. We'll need the bullets I brought now that the FBI knows some of you are carrying blanks."

Becca couldn't see them, but everyone in the library could hear them.

"How did they find out?" Frank asked.

"Beats me," Craig said. "But you should all load up with them. I've got plenty to go around."

"Frank! Troy isn't looking too good." Dale's voice was panicked. "I think his knee is broken. His nose, too."

"Let me take a look."

Seconds later, Troy roared in pain. Then he spit out a string of curses. "Give me something for the pain! Dale, give me some of your meds."

Abigail narrowed her eyes at Becca, throwing a lethal look that no one else seemed to catch. "They'll probably punish her for that also, hurting one of them."

"How did *she* manage to take down the big guy?" Nolan asked.

"Beats me." Abigail shrugged, playing clueless. "Maybe she takes classes at the self-defense school that woman owns. What's it called?"

"USD," Tyler said in a low voice.

As a matter of fact, Becca did take classes at the Underground Self-Defense School to keep the skills she'd acquired and built upon since college honed. That woman who owned it was Charlie Sharp. She made a great sparring partner because she was formidable and far from easy to take down.

Someone approached the story time room with keys jangling.

Frank unlocked the door and stuck his head in. "Tyler and Abigail, you're going to be released."

No. That would give Abigail an opportunity to disappear. She would get away with her part in this.

"What about me?" Nolan asked.

"What about you? Once we get the money, we'll let you and that one—" Frank pointed a finger at Becca "—go. It'll be a while, so in the meantime, we're going to move the troublemaker upstairs. Change things up a bit since the FBI might know we were keeping you in here."

Jake had done it. He'd negotiated her release. But what about the others?

"And me?" Hope filled Cameron's voice.

"Unless your father does the right thing, we move forward with the plan. Don't worry. We've got more lidocaine."

EVERYONE HAD LEAPED into action, getting their Hail Mary pass cleared, the app loaded on Jake's phone as well as gaining access to stream on the FBI's official YouTube channel. Between Jake, Nash and Aaron, they'd made it happen in less than an hour. Having one of their own as a hostage galvanized the higher-ups, allowing them to cut through the bureaucratic red tape of trying this unorthodox approach.

Sheriff Clark had announced to media that the hostage taker in charge would make a statement on the FBI's channel.

After Jake had ordered SWAT to stand down and contacted Frank again, he was ready to go. Frank was prepared to release two more hostages and was waiting for him.

Jake handed Nash his holstered weapon. He put his Swiss Army knife on the desk, wishing he could take it with him if for no other reason than luck. But they'd consider it a weapon, confiscate it, and then there would be no way to regain Frank's trust and end this peacefully. Better to leave behind his favorite, multipurpose tool.

Putting comms in his ear, Jake left the trailer along with Nash.

Lund approached them. "See, I knew those animals were bluffing and wouldn't hurt my son."

His arrogance knew no bounds.

"They weren't bluffing," Jake said, noticing Father O'Neill speaking to Mrs. Lund off to the side. "We bought Cameron six hours. Do what you can to expedite the wire transfer if you care anything at all about your son's life."

Lund was opening his mouth to spout more hot air.

Fortunately, Nash stepped between them, giving Jake a chance to make his exit.

Hustling around the command center, he raised his palms once he reached the street. He darted across Seventh over to the open window.

"Hang on a second," Frank said, hidden inside. "Take it nice and slow."

Jake crept closer across the lawn to the window.

"Stop," Frank ordered. "We're sending out Tyler and Abigail."

A teenager with curly blond hair emerged first. "Tyler?"

"Yes, sir." The boy wasted no time making his way up to the window.

Jake got him out of the building and directed him where to run. Next the older woman with salt-and-pepper hair that he'd seen before hurried into the office. She climbed up onto the desk, moving like she had stiffness or arthritis in her legs. He took her hand and helped her put one leg at a time over the ledge, then eased her down to the grass.

"Agents are waiting for you at the trailer."

"Thank you. God bless you." Turning, Abigail scurried toward the trailer.

"Okay, now you come in, slowly," Frank said. "No sudden moves. We'll pat you down once you're inside."

"I'm going in," Jake said over comms to Nash and Utley. "Remember, no one fires a shot unless I give the green light."

"Roger that," Utley replied. "None of my guys will pull a trigger without your clearance."

Putting his hands on the ledge of the window, Jake hopped up. He planted a foot, hunched down and climbed into the office.

"Close and lock the window," Frank said. "Then come this way with your hands up."

Jake did as he was instructed, shutting the window first. Raising his palms high in the air, he eased forward.

Once he reached the doorway, someone grabbed the collar of his jacket and pulled him off to the side out of view from the window.

Frank pointed a gun at him. "We didn't expect you to find out that we were using blank cartridges."

One foot separated them. Close enough range for that round to cause real damage, even potentially kill him. A blank didn't have a slug, but it still had an explosive charge.

"Since you know," Frank added, "it turned out to be a good thing that Craig brought live rounds. I've got a few loaded in here." He waved the Glock. "I hope I don't have to use it. But if you test me, I will."

"Fair enough."

A second man, older and shorter, stepped forward. Dale McKee. "Keep those hands lifted while I search you." He proceeded to pat Jake down roughly, lifting his FBI jacket, and going so far as to check his groin as well as his ankles.

"You were very thorough," Jake said.

"I wasn't about to let you sneak a weapon in here." Dale handed him his phone.

Jake took the cell and lowered his hands. "I need

to see Agent Becca Hammond before we can start the live stream."

"Okay," Frank said. "Follow Dale."

The other man led the way down the hall. Frank walked behind Jake, keeping the gun leveled at his head. Inside the building, it was hot as an oven. The air was stale and far too arid. The daytime temperature hadn't even reached its peak yet.

"You need to give the hostages at the entrances water," Jake said. "Give them a chance to use the restroom."

Frank pressed the muzzle of the gun against the back of his skull. "We'd be too exposed by those front doors. You want them to have water and a potty break? Then we need the money and the evidence."

"What good is the money if you're dead or in jail?" Jake asked.

"I never said the money was for us. We've got loved ones who could use it. There are a lot of folks in this town who are still hurting, suffering from the Plainsman accident," Frank said. "The ones who died left their families drowning in debt. Split twenty-seven ways, no one is getting rich, but folks will be able to subsist. We're not greedy. Just looking to do right by those who were wronged."

Jake suspected there was something odd about them asking for six and a half million. Now he understood why.

They reached the main area of the library. Troy Sims sat at the information desk, looking as if he had been through a knock-down-drag-out fight and lost. He moaned in pain, unable to sit still. His leg was propped up in a chair. The pant leg had been cut, revealing a badly swollen knee that was possibly broken. Holding a blood-soaked towel up to his nose with his left hand, he held his right against his chest, like it was also injured. It would be hard for the man to grip a gun, not that Jake spotted one within the man's reach.

"Looks like your buddy needs medical attention," Jake said.

Frank grunted. "Thanks to that FBI agent."

Becca's handiwork. She had rendered the biggest one useless.

"I'd be happy to escort him out of here and get him some," Jake offered.

"I'm staying, Frank," Troy mumbled as he shifted in his seat, his face spasming in agony. "I just need some more pills for the pain."

"Any more will make you sleepy," Dale said.

Troy groaned. "I could use a break from the pain. Please. Just one more."

Dale took a medicine bottle out of his pocket and popped a pill in Troy's palm. The big guy swallowed it without water.

From the schematic of the building, he knew where the story time room was located. Jake eased around the desk until it came into view. Through the glass window he saw Cameron Lund and Russell Nolan sitting on the floor.

But no Becca.

"Where is she?" Jake asked.

"Figured you'd be expecting her in there." Frank gestured to the story time room. "In case you had something planned, we moved her."

"Where?"

"Let's get your agent out here," Frank said. "Walk."

Dale strode ahead and Jake followed him to a staircase that led to the second floor. Bright sunlight poured in through windows. SWAT had told him there had been movement on the stairs earlier while they were making preparations for the livestream. There hadn't been time for them to take a shot and they had wanted to know if they got another opportunity what they should do.

His response was the same as before. Hold all fire.

"Craig!" Frank called. "Bring her out."

A door opened somewhere on the second floor. Footsteps clacked down the stairs. At the landing, Craig appeared with Becca, the sunlight framing her like she was angel. Craig held her elbow, a gun pointed at her side.

She was restrained, hands behind her back, and gagged with duct tape over her mouth. Craig shepherded her down the next flight of stairs, bringing her closer. They stopped midway on the steps.

An uneasy feeling stirred in Jake's gut. Why was she gagged? "I need to speak with her," he said. "You'll need to remove the duct tape."

"Not happening." Frank moved from behind Jake to the side of him. "You see she's fine. You can still speak to her. Ask yes or no questions. She'll be able to respond."

What Jake wouldn't have given to have a moment alone with her. To hold her. Reassure her that he was doing absolutely everything in his power to get her out of this.

"Have they hurt you?" Jake asked.

Becca's gaze shifted to the man who had a tight grip on her—the one who had hit her—but then she shook her head *no*.

"Are you all right?"

She gave him a curt nod. Fatigue and possibly dehydration darkened the skin beneath her eyes. Still, she was the most beautiful woman he'd ever seen.

"Have they given you enough water?"

Lowering her gaze as if weary, she shook her head.

"Take off the tape. Give her some water and food," Jake demanded. "Look at her. She's dehydrated and starving."

"She'll get water and a snack," Frank said. "After I say my piece for the world to hear."

Craig narrowed his eyes. "What are you talking about?"

"Agent Delgado is going to put me up on the FBI's YouTube channel. Live. With all the news outlets watching. I'm going to tell them all everything about Lund. Isn't that right, Jake?"

"Oh, no, you're not." Craig's tone hardened. "We discussed this already. I'm sick and tired of hearing you go on and on about justice. There's no such thing for folks like us. We need to get the money first! You go spouting off to the media and Lund might decide *not* to pay. People are counting on us. Make your statement after the money hits the account."

"What if Lund doesn't follow through? What if he

has no intention of paying?" Frank asked. "We have a chance. Granted, it's not like I had envisioned it, but streaming live on the FBI's channel with all the major outlets recording it, to tell the truth about what happened."

"You don't listen! But you're going to." Craig jammed his weapon deeper into Becca's side, making her wince. He threw his other arm around her throat and started climbing back up the stairs, taking her with him. "No interview, or statement, or whatever the hell he's planning," Craig said, staring at Jake. "Got it? Otherwise, I'll hurt her." He took three more steps up. "Do you hear me? Frank has to wait until after we've got confirmation of the money in the account. Understand!" Another three and they were exposed to the window again.

Dread balled up in Jake's chest.

In his ear, Utley's voice came over the comms. "We have a visual. We can take a shot. How to proceed?"

Jake tapped the Bluetooth device. "Hold your fire. I repeat. Do not shoot."

"What are you doing?" Dale asked his cohort, following them up the stairs.

Craig tightened his grip on Becca's throat, making her eyes flare wide. "I'm giving the orders for once. You should be backing me on this."

Frank kept his gun trained on Jake, but his attention was on Craig.

"We can't hurt an FBI agent," Dale pleaded. "Let Frank make his statement. It's all set up and arranged."

"You knew he was planning this?" Disbelief contorted Craig's features. "After that stunt with the bull-horn? We agreed it was a bad idea."

"No, we didn't." Dale shook his head, drawing closer. His voice was calm, his cadence slow. "We heard you out, but we didn't agree. This has to be about more than money. Lund needs to be punished. Hannah is going to teach him a lesson. Make him regret what he did. But Frank needs to make a statement so that the world needs to understand why she's going to—"

A crack sounded in the air. The bullet pierced the window, hitting Dale in the head. Almost in slow motion, he crumpled, sinking to his knees, and rolled down the steps.

Jake's pulse scrambled. "Don't shoot," he said over comms. Becca could be hit. Craig was losing it. The guy had the muzzle of his gun pressed into her side. His finger could slip, and he could accidentally shoot her. "Hold your fire."

"That wasn't us," Utley responded.

Oh, God.

Then who was firing?

Cold fear replaced his worry.

Craig turned, swinging his gun toward the broken window, still holding on tight to Becca.

Frank stood frozen, staring at Dale, dead on the floor.

Moving fast, Jake spun and took hold of the Glock, one finger thrust behind the trigger so it wouldn't go off, and twisted the gun from Frank's hand. Jake pivoted as another crack sounded.

The second bullet struck Craig, the impact knocking

him backward. Down the staircase. Taking her along with him.

Jake's heart rocketed into his throat.

Becca!

Their bodies tumbled down the steps in a tangle until they finally hit the bottom. A bullet to the head had killed Craig. Becca hadn't been hit.

But she was unconscious.

No, no, no. Horror screamed through Jake.

"Two down," he said over comms, running to her. "Breach the library! Move in now! I need medical. Agent down." Jake made sure to keep Frank in his sights, turning the gun on him. "Get down. On your belly. Hands clasped behind your head."

Stunned, Frank complied without a word.

Jake crouched beside Becca, moving her away from the dead man, who thankfully hadn't landed on top of her. He put two shaky fingers to her carotid artery. His heart nearly stopped as he felt for a pulse.

She had one. It was thready, but there.

Quickly but gently, he pulled the duct tape from her mouth, hoping it would help her to breathe easier. If only he had his Swiss Army knife to cut the zip tie.

"Wake up, Becca."

Please open your eyes. Please, his mind begged.

Where in the hell were the medics?

Chapter Thirteen

The GPS chimed. A digital voice said, "You have reached your destination."

Brian parked. He had already interviewed the Compassionate Hearts charity, questioned the transportation manager for Plainsman Oil and Gas, brought the Lunds to the command center, searched Craig Hicks's house and spoken to one of the car owners whose license plates had been stolen, which had led nowhere.

One more owner to interview.

Breaking news came over the radio. He turned it up.

"The library invasion turned lockdown has ended after twenty-two grueling hours," said a local reporter. "All of the hostages have been released. Two of the captors were killed. Although SWAT is denying responsibility for the shots that claimed their lives. The other two, who have been identified as Frank Ferguson and Troy Sims, are in police custody. A hostage was rushed from the scene in an ambulance. The person has yet to be identified. Many other hostages are being treated for heat exhaustion and dehydration. Here comes Crispin Lund now. Mr. Lund, how does it feel to have your son safely returned to you by the joint efforts of the FBI and the sheriff's department?"

"Although they did their best, you give them too much credit. I always knew this would be the outcome," Lund said over the radio, his voice triumphant. "My son, Cameron, back with his family, unharmed, and those animals not getting one red cent from me. To the ones who are still alive, I hope you rot in prison."

Rolling his eyes, Brian shut off the radio. For a moment, he considered simply returning to the command center. But he was all about dotting his *i*'s and crossing his *t*'s. Once he started down a road, he had to see it through to completion. Nothing pleased him more than filling in the blanks. Well, nothing beside catching the bad guys.

Brian cut the engine, got out of the car and climbed the steps to the house. He knocked. After waiting a minute with no answer, he glanced at the sedan in the driveway and knocked again. Louder this time.

Footsteps approached. The door swung open. Lo and behold, it was Goldilocks.

"Hello. Again," Brian said, surprised.

She grinned. "Hello, Detective. Are you stalking me?"

"No, ma'am." His cheeks heated. "Are you Hannah Hayes?"

"Yes, I am. What can I do for you?"

"Did you file a police report that your license plates were stolen?"

"Sure did. Hope you're here to tell me you caught the guy."

Brian gave a low chuckle. "The men have been apprehended, but that's not why I'm here. Do you mind if I step inside a moment? I have some questions for you."

Hannah glanced over her shoulder like she was considering it. Then she looked back at him. "Come on in." She opened the door wide.

He stepped inside.

After closing the door, she led him into the living room. "Do you think you're going to be here long enough for coffee?"

He had already exceeded his limit for the day, but there was still paperwork to complete well into the night. "Sure, if it's not too much trouble."

"No trouble at all." Hannah smiled. The pigtails made her look like someone straight out of a fairy tale. "I can even rustle up a few chocolate chip cookies if you like. It's the premade ready-to-bake kind. They'd be warm and done by the time the coffee is, if I pop them in the air fryer."

Wow. She was too good to be true. "The air fryer, huh?"

"It's a hack. No need to waste time preheating an oven. They come out a little crispy on the outside, but soft and chewy on the inside."

Sounded delicious. "Thank you, ma'am. I haven't had lunch and a sweet pick-me-up would really hit the spot."

"Coming right up. So long as you stop calling me ma'am. It's Hannah."

Smiling at her again, he took off his cowboy hat and placed it on the coffee table. He started heading to the kitchen behind her. "We can speak while you're getting everything ready."

"No, no," she said, spinning around with a palm raised, stopping him. She had thin, long, delicate fingers. Fine bone structure. "You take a seat right over there." She pointed to the sofa on the other side of the room. "Give me a minute and then you can have my undivided attention."

His mother hated him being underfoot in the kitchen, too. He simply appreciated the hospitality. "Okay." Turning, he took out his cell phone. He called the command center to check in.

"Agent Vance."

"This is Brian. I'm interviewing one more person about the stolen plates."

"Moot point. We've got 'em. Two dead. Two in custody."

"The only holes I like are the ones in doughnuts." His stomach grumbled. "How's Becca doing?" He was sure she was thrilled to be out of that library.

"She fell down the stairs when one of the perps was taken out. Right now, she's unconscious at the hospital," Aaron said. "Jake is with her in the emergency room."

What the hell? "I heard something on the radio about SWAT saying they didn't take the shots."

"Correct. Commander Utley is confident it wasn't one of his men. They're saying the two shots fired originated about a hundred meters behind them from a different rooftop."

"Did anyone ever locate Lund's head of security?" Brian asked. One minute the creepy dude was there. The next he was gone.

"Not that I know of."

"That might be a good place to start looking for our unidentified shooter. I know he was prior service. Marine Corps. But I have no idea what his specialty was." Something told Brian that it involved killing people.

"Fire off a quick email with essentials, things you know for certain and anything you suspect. I'll dig into him."

"On it," Brian said. "When there's any news about Becca, please let me know." As soon as she was awake, he intended to head to the hospital.

"You got it."

Brian disconnected. He pulled up his email, typed a few lines of what he knew about Lund's head of security, including the vibe he got from the man.

Hannah waltzed out of the kitchen and looked at him expectantly. "The coffee and cookies will be done momentarily."

"One minute," he said, wrapping up the email. He hit send. "Okay, that's taken care of."

Smiling, she sat in a chair that faced the sofa. "How can I help you, Detective?" She gestured for him to sit.

"Call me Brian." He took a seat on the couch. "When did you notice that your license plates were missing?"

"Um, I believe it was in the morning. The day I filed the report." She rubbed her hands together as she spoke. "I was getting ready to head to Compassionate Hearts. I volunteer over there a few hours a week."

Hospitable and altruistic. "What do you do for a living?"

"I'm a data security analyst. It sounds fairly dull when I discuss it, but I love the work."

Smart, too. "Can you run me through what you were doing the day prior to the theft?"

"Well, let me think," she said, her gaze veering to the ceiling, "I went to Compassionate Hearts in the morning, and I was there for about four hours."

"I doubt the plates were taken then. The parking lot faces the store and a main road." Though it did make him wonder whether this was a coincidence. Hannah volunteering at the same charity where the vans were stolen as well as being one of the owners of the plates that were used in the crime. "What did you do next?"

"Went shopping. I got some supplies from the big-box store off Grand Avenue."

"Depending on how busy the store was that day, they might have been taken then. Do you remember where you parked in the lot? Whether there was heavy traffic?"

"I always park on the far end. To get my steps in." She flashed those pearly whites. "The traffic was light. Plenty of open spaces."

Parked away from the store with light traffic might have presented the perfect opportunity for the plates to be lifted. "When you came out of the store, can you say for certain if the license plates were still there?" he asked. The smell of chocolate chip cookies permeating the air made his stomach grumble.

"Um, I can't really say. I was on the phone. Not really paying attention."

"Did you put your bags in the trunk or inside the car?"

"In the car, passenger's seat."

"After that, did you go anywhere else or straight home?"

Beeps came from the kitchen. "That's the timer." She stood. "I had a late lunch with my godfather at the Cast Iron Grill."

Brian was familiar with it. There weren't any cameras in the parking lot for him to verify whether or not her plates were on the car when she arrived and left.

"Then I came home." She headed to the kitchen and disappeared inside.

Although his interest in stone-cold Charlie Sharp never waned, he couldn't help but be intrigued by Hannah. She seemed like a wonderful woman.

Standing, he glanced around the living room, taking it in. "How long have you volunteered at Compassionate Hearts?" The furniture was well worn and comfortable. Several pieces might have even come from the charity shop. The walls were a soft, neutral gray.

"A couple of years," she said, dishes clinking. "Ever since I moved back home to Laramie."

Instead of art on the walls, photographs were hung in a decorative pattern with frames in varying sizes, shapes and materials. "Why did you leave?"

"For college. I attended Cornell University. Full scholarship."

So, she was really smart.

He drifted to the artful display. "In upstate New York, right?"

"Yup. Ithaca."

"What brought you back here?" he asked, looking over the photos.

"Family. They needed me. I thought that if I could help, I should."

Based on the pictures, it seemed as though she'd had a happy childhood. He came across several of her with Abigail Abshire. One of the former hostages.

A ball of unease settled like a rock in the pit of his stomach.

Was this yet another coincidence?

The charity where the vans had been stolen, her license plates taken and used during the crime, now this.

Brian was about to ask Hannah if she was related to Abigail, but another picture stopped him cold.

It was of a barbecue or a cookout. Hannah stood beside Frank Ferguson, with his arm around her shoulders, Dale McKee and a woman he didn't recognize. In the background was Abigail Abshire again, Dennis McKee and others, including the proprietor of the gun shop who had refused to give Brian access to his surveillance footage. Below that one was another of Hannah wearing her graduation cap and gown for college, surrounded by people who were clearly proud of her. Frank was in that one, too, hugging her so tight, like she was his daughter. And another with her as a little girl, maybe ten years old, same curly blond hair and bright blue eyes.

The knot in his gut tightened.

"Where did you say you worked?" Brian asked, putting his hand on the hilt of his weapon.

"I didn't."

A floorboard creaked. His gaze flew from the picture to the kitchen doorway.

Holding a tray of coffee and cookies, Hannah stood frozen, eyes wide, looking like a deer caught in headlights. She glanced at the photo he'd been eyeing. Then her gaze fell to where his hand gripped the hilt of his weapon.

The tray fell from her hands in a clatter to the floor. Whirling, she darted back into the kitchen.

Brian took off after her, drawing his firearm. As he crossed the threshold, she whipped out a weapon from her purse on the counter. Hannah swung around and aimed.

But not at him.

By the time he realized she was targeting the laptop, he glimpsed a countdown on the screen.

She pulled the trigger, putting four bullets into the computer.

"Drop your weapon! Hands in the air!"

Hannah let go of the gun, letting it hit the floor and raised her palms.

Brian inched closer, kicked her weapon away and holstered his gun before slipping handcuffs on her wrists.

Making sure the cuffs were tight, he looked past the pigtails, down at her pretty face. "You and I are going to have a different conversation. In the interrogation room down at the sheriff's department."

"It doesn't matter. It's too late now. There's nothing you or anyone else can do to stop it."

"Stop what?" he asked, everything inside of him warning that her answer was going to mean serious trouble.

Hannah smiled, but there was a vicious gleam in her eyes, almost feral. "The payback Lund deserves."

Chapter Fourteen

The darkness receded, ebbing like the tide away from shore. Becca opened her eyes. She squinted against the harsh, bright light.

Fluorescent bulbs flickered overhead. The smell of antiseptic hit her nose. Scratchy sheets. Stiff bed. A machine beeped, and something wrapped around her arm squeezed her bicep. Gasping, she jerked and reached out, clawing at it.

"Hey, there," a deep voice murmured. "Becca, it's fine. It's a blood pressure cuff." Jake leaned over the bed and stared down at her.

She had never been so happy to see his handsome face.

"Blood pressure?" Becca looked around, her surroundings registering. She was in a room in the hospital. Alarm had her jerking fully awake. The cuff didn't loosen on her arm as a line leading from a needle to her vein tugged at her skin. "What happened?"

"Someone shot Dale McKee. Then Craig Hicks while that bastard still had his arm wrapped around your throat. The force of shot propelled him backward. You took a nasty fall. Could've broken your neck."

"I'm surprised SWAT would take such a risky shot."

Jake shook his head. "They didn't. It was an unidentified shooter."

That sounded ominous. "Any ideas who it might have been?"

"My money is on someone from Lund's security team. He was the one with the most to lose."

"What about Frank and Troy?"

"Both arrested. Troy is here in the hospital being treated. Deputies are assigned to watch him. You did one heck of a number on him."

The fight came back to her in a rush that got her adrenaline going. An altercation that could have been avoided if she hadn't been betrayed. "Abigail Abshire was working with Frank and the others."

"Really?" He shook his head in disbelief. "But they used her as a human shield when it all started. Troy Sims held her in front of him with a gun pointed at her. It was the reason I couldn't take a shot."

"It was all an act. The entire time she pretended to be a hostage. She told them I had the phone. That I was calling you. Someone needs to find her and bring her in."

"I'll let Nash know."

Sitting up, Becca unwrapped the blood pressure cuff from her arm.

"What are you doing?" Alarm shot across his face.

"What does it look like I'm doing?" Thankfully, she

hadn't been in the emergency room long enough for them to deem it necessary to change her out of her clothes and into a gown. She spotted her boots on a nearby chair, propped on top of her small overnight bag. "I'm fine."

She did feel much better since the library. Less dizzy and hot than she had in those terrifying moments when she had been standing on the landing of the staircase. Shots fired. Falling before everything had gone black.

Shoving the memory aside, she started to pull off the tape that was holding down the needle to the IV.

"You're not fine." He clamped a hand over hers, stopping her. "You've been out cold for a bit."

Maybe that was the reason they were monitoring her blood pressure and had given her an IV.

"I've been sitting here worried sick." His voice rumbled with frustration and something that sounded like fear. "Waiting for answers. Waiting for you to open your eyes." Concern etched into his expression. "You're going to stay put until the doctor clears you." He pressed a palm to her cheek, and she couldn't help but turn into his touch.

The affection beaming in his hazel eyes warmed her to the core, stunning her into silence. For once, she didn't fight him. "Has the doctor said anything?" she asked.

"The nurse took blood from you to run tests." Jake lowered his palm from her face and held her hand between his. "They also did a CT scan on you."

His gaze fell. He was pale, his brow furrowed.

Was he that worried about her?

She lifted a hand, wanting to run her fingers through his hair, but there was a knock at the door, stopping her.

A man with sandy-blond hair, wearing green scrubs, entered the room. "Glad to see you're finally awake. I'm Dr. Plinsky. Would you like your friend to step outside while we speak privately?"

"I'm not going anywhere," Jake said.

The doctor frowned at him. "Because you're both federal agents and she was injured during an investigation, we've allowed you to sit with her. But according to the forms you filled out, you're not a family member." Dr. Plinsky cut his gaze from him. "Agent Hammond, this is your decision. I can have Agent Delgado escorted to the waiting room by security if need be."

"No, no." Becca shook her head. "That won't be necessary. I'd like for him to stay."

Whatever the doctor told her, she would share with him anyway. He might as well hear it firsthand.

"Are you sure?" the doctor asked. "The nature of what I need to tell you is sensitive. You might want privacy."

"I'm pregnant," Becca blurted out.

"Yes, ma'am." Dr. Plinsky nodded with a faint smile. "According to the test results, you are."

Jake sucked in a breath like there was suddenly less oxygen in the room. As though he'd forgotten about the baby until forced to remember.

The nights that they had been together at her place, when she'd shared precious pieces of her life, had been the closest that she'd ever gotten to showing any other person, outside of her family, the deepest part of her heart. Now she understood that he hadn't realized what those moments had meant.

She pulled her hand from his.

"We've ruled out a concussion. Your CT scan was good. We believe you passed out from a combination of things. The fall, dehydration, low blood sugar as well as low blood pressure. With the IV, you should be feeling better."

"Yes, I am."

"You should try to eat something soon. How have you been doing with holding down food? Much morning sickness?"

She swallowed. "Quite a bit actually, that lasts until midday."

"That'll get better once you're out of your first trimester." The confidence in Dr. Plinsky's tone was reassuring.

"How far along is she?" Jake asked. "When is the baby due?"

Dr. Plinsky looked to her as though she had the answers.

"I only found out recently. Home pregnancy test." Becca stared at her clasped hands. "My best guess is eight weeks."

"Based on you HCG levels," the doctor said, "that's about right."

"HCG?" Jake asked, and Becca wondered as well.

"Human chorionic gonadotropin is a hormone produced by the placenta. The levels can tell us a lot, but an ultrasound will show more. Since you haven't had one yet, I suggest we do one."

"I'm meeting with an ob-gyn next week," Becca said. "Can it wait until then?"

"I wouldn't advise waiting. Because you're of advanced maternal age, you run a higher risk for complications. We should do a viability ultrasound now."

Fear jolted through her. "What?" She exchanged an alarmed glance with Jake.

"Advanced maternal age? Viability?" he asked, taking the words from her mouth. "Becca's only thirty-six. Why wouldn't the baby be viable?"

The doctor sighed. "Any pregnancy where the birthing person is older than thirty-five is considered advanced maternal age. Older mothers are predisposed to enormous adverse outcomes, like miscarriage, congenital disorders, high blood pressure," he said, making Becca's head spin again. "A lot can happen in the early stages of a pregnancy. I think we should do an ultrasound and go from there."

If she were the only parent in the room, she would've screamed, *Yes, do it now.* But she wasn't. She looked at Jake, not sure if wanted to be a part of this on any level, needing to give him a chance to punch out.

The uncertainty in his face broke her heart.

"Why don't I give you a minute to think about it? I'm going to grab something from the vending machine. Would you like anything?" the doctor asked her.

"Pretzels. Or something starchy and salty." Chips would do.

"Coming right up." Dr. Plinsky flashed a grin before heading out of the room, closing the door behind him.

Becca hated this. Loving someone. Desperate to have them love her back and want the life she wanted.

Her mother had gone through that. Becca and Clare had watched her suffer for years after their father walked away, abandoning them. As a little girl, she'd sworn that she would never go through that.

It was better for her to know where she stood with him, accept and move on.

She wanted Jake, but she didn't need him.

Becca had enough love for herself and this child.

JAKE HAD NO clue how to navigate something of this magnitude, but he was smart enough to know that whatever he said or did next would be locked away in Becca's memory bank forever.

"What are you thinking?" she asked. "How do you feel about doing the ultrasound?"

He shrugged and blew out a breath. "I don't know."

Jake was still processing the prospect of a baby. What if the ultrasound showed it wasn't viable? Then what were they supposed to do?

It was a "no news was good news" scenario for him.

"Figures," she snapped. "I can raise this baby on my own. I've got my sister and my mom here to help me. I don't need you. Consider yourself off the hook." She smoothed her hands down the bedsheet. "There's no reason for you to hang around."

"Off the hook? Are you serious?" He reeled from the cold words. "I'd support any child of mine."

"I don't need a check from you."

That came out all wrong. As usual, when it involved Becca.

He pressed a palm to his forehead. "How long have you known that you're pregnant?"

Crossing her arms over her chest, she said, "A week."

He groaned, disappointment flooding him.

They had spoken over the phone four times in the past week. It had all been work-related, but still, four missed opportunities for her to share the news. To give him a chance to wrap his head around it and determine an appropriate response.

Getting hot under the collar, he hopped to his feet. "You've known for a week, had time to sort through your feelings, and then decide to drag me all the way from Denver to drop the bombshell on me. Can I have some time to process it? I'm not asking for a week, but at least a few days."

Becca rolled her eyes, stiffening. "You don't want to be a husband. You don't want to be a father. You don't want this. When we first started having *fun* together, you made that crystal clear. Am I wrong?"

No, she wasn't, and he didn't have the heart to say it.

But while she was held captive, something had loosened inside him, in his heart. Like pieces of a puzzle that he was putting together. He couldn't quite articulate it yet.

"The second I saw the positive symbol on the home

pregnancy test I wanted this baby," she said, her voice low and sad. "I didn't know how I was going to be a mother and an agent and be good at both, but I wanted it. You don't. And that's okay. You didn't sign up for a lifetime obligation. We both agreed to casual and easy. I'm sorry that somewhere along the way it changed for me while it was just sex for you."

Shaking his head, he squeezed his eyes shut. He didn't want a failed marriage because they were long distance, both focused on work and fighting all the time. He didn't want to be a failure as a father because he only saw his kid every other weekend, during the summers and alternating holidays.

His mother had quit her job and stayed at home.

That was not a choice Becca Hammond would ever make. To even imply it would get him cut down with laser beams from her eyes.

Ironically, that was what attracted him to Becca. Her guts. Her strength. Her determination. Her fiery independence.

He didn't know how to make it work. How to juggle it all. God, it sounded like she didn't, either.

They would be disastrous together.

Plinsky walked back in, holding up a bag of pretzels and a protein bar for her. "You need both."

"My hero," she said, taking the food.

Jake glanced at her with narrowed eyes, befuddled by her choice of words.

"So, what did you decide?" the doctor asked. "Are

we doing the ultrasound? Which I strongly recommend for the health of mother and child."

How could he say no? Even he wanted to, which he didn't, it would not go over very well.

"Yes, let's do it," Jake said. He needed to make sure Becca and the baby were okay. That the fetus was viable.

To share seeing the baby for the first time with her was a once-in-a-lifetime chance he didn't want to miss. She would always remember it and hate him if he wasn't a willing participant.

The doctor looked at Becca, and she nodded.

"Pull your dress up, exposing your belly," Plinsky instructed.

As Becca did, he noticed her hands trembling slightly. She settled back on the bed, with her lower half covered by the sheet.

She had the kind of body that could break a man. He wondered what she would look like with her belly full and round, heavy with his child. Probably even sexier.

The doctor squirted goo on her abdomen. Becca gasped.

"Sorry that it's cold," he said.

She smiled. "It's okay."

The doctor pressed the probe to her belly and moved it around while staring at the screen until a weird throbbing noise echoed in the room as an indecipherable image flickered on the screen.

"That's your baby's heartbeat," Plinsky said to Becca, and she beamed.

It was so fast. Jake listened closer. "Is that normal? It's like a hundred and forty per minute."

"You have a very good ear." The doctor grinned. "It's one forty-five."

"Is everything okay?" Jake asked, hating the strain in his voice.

"Very normal. Very healthy." The doctor pointed to the peanut-shaped outline on the screen. "There's the baby. You can see the heart beating."

Becca gasped, grinning from ear to ear.

Jake was awestruck. It was so tiny. So fragile. All his fears and concerns snowballed.

"I would say that you're eight weeks, almost nine. Due date is February. Close to Valentine's Day."

Pressing both hands to her chest, she stared at the monitor.

Questions ricocheted in his head like a steel ball bearing in pinball machine. "What does this mean for lifestyle changes that she needs to make?"

Becca glared at him.

"She should start taking a prenatal vitamin every day," the doctor said. "Besides that it's the usual, adequate nutrition. Cut back on salt, fat, sugar. No alcohol. No caffeine. Be sure to stay hydrated and get proper rest."

"She has a physically demanding job," Jake said, his concerns overwhelming him. "Would it be best for her to take safer assignments where she's sitting at desk all the time?"

"What?" Indignation cut through her voice, slashing across her face. "Can't I continue to do my job, as well as exercise, Doctor?"

Plinsky sucked in a breath. "Rebecca is pregnant. Not disabled. I would highly encourage her to continue exercising and doing her job, especially if she enjoys it. Now, once you're well into your second trimester, you might want to slow down. I wouldn't recommend that you run after a criminal and detain him at that late stage. Pregnancy is an adjustment. Just like parenthood. But a manageable one that could change your life for the better." He shut off the machine and handed Becca some paper towels. "I'm going to discharge you. Eat up, stay hydrated, and most importantly, keep being you."

"Her job is dangerous," Jake said. "She could get hurt. The baby could. Shouldn't she at least spend the night for observation?"

"Unbelievable." Becca shook her head with a look of disgust.

"Anybody could get hurt, anywhere, any time. That goes for an FBI agent, regardless of gender, or whether they're pregnant. Her OB will monitor her closely because of her age to make sure she doesn't have any issues with gestational diabetes, preeclampsia or preterm labor. The best way for her to avoid depression and anxiety is to continue her routine."

"Which is high stress and causes anxiety?" Jake asked, flummoxed. "She thrives off it, but it can't be good for the baby."

"I won't debate this with you, sir," Plinsky said, firmly. "As long as she's healthy, any doctor will clear her to continue doing her job." He looked at Becca. "Mother and baby are healthy. Prenatal vitamins. Hydrate. Eat. Sleep. Got it?"

She nodded. Her earlier enthusiasm deflated.

Because of Jake.

The doctor left.

Becca wiped the goo off her belly with the paper towel, tossed back the covers and stood. "That was humiliating on so many levels. This could've been an incredible moment for us. A breakthrough. Instead, it was…more of the same," she said, her chest heaving, "you doubting me. You questioning my judgment. You treating me like…" Tears welled in her eyes. She ripped the tape from her arm and pulled out the IV. Grabbing her boots and the overnight bag he'd packed for her, she stormed to the attached bathroom and slammed the door.

Jake took a deep breath, hating that he'd upset her.

He could attest to the fact that any agent could get hurt at any time. He'd seen it all. But this was different.

This was Becca. The mother of his child.

The toilet flushed. The water ran for a while. Finally, she emerged from the bathroom, wearing fresh clothes. Jeans, T-shirt, sneakers.

"I'm sorry." He stood and crossed the room, closing the space between them. "It's just that I don't want you in harm's way. Pregnant. Or not. I care about you. I don't want anything to happen to you."

"Ditto." She met his gaze. "But I wouldn't ask you not to do your job. Because I also respect you."

"Becca," he said, shaking his head. "What I feel for you far exceeds respect. Goes so much deeper." He wanted to say more. To tell her how impressed he had been with the way she had handled herself, how grateful he was that she was alive and well. Both her and the baby. He looked down into her beautiful face, and instead of speaking his mind, he put his hands on her waist and pulled her against him.

In a heartbeat, his prized control splintered, and his mouth came down on hers.

Becca stiffened, for a split second, but then her lips softened under his. Her palms slid over his chest as she kissed him back.

She tasted like heaven, and the desire he'd been fighting broke free.

Jake deepened the kiss, turning it wet and hot and pouring every emotion he hadn't voiced into it. Becca returned the passion full measure.

Lust pumped like a drug through his veins and his groin tightened. But it was more than that. Something greater flared in his heart as well. A feeling he didn't quite recognize swelled inside him.

Then he realized it was hope.

She made him believe that a relationship and a family were possible despite the odds saying otherwise. Or the fact that they had no plan.

Hope was dangerous. It was also beautiful.

Becca had invaded his life like a force he never saw coming, and now he couldn't imagine being without her.

He just didn't want to let her down.

Someone coughed, loudly from the doorway.

They separated, collecting themselves.

"We were worried." Brian strolled into the room. "It's good to see you up and at 'em."

"Thanks," she said, blushing.

Brian grimaced. "I hate to be the bearer of bad news, but—"

"What is it?" Becca asked.

"We've got a problem," Brian said. "A big one. This thing with Frank Ferguson, McKee and the others— this vendetta they have—isn't over. I think the worst is yet to come."

Chapter Fifteen

At the sheriff's department, they stood huddled in the observation room that had one-way glass overlooking the adjacent interrogation room.

Munching on a bag of roasted almonds, Becca stared at Hannah Hayes. Niece of Abigail Hayes Abshire, who was in the wind, hiding out somewhere. Goddaughter to Frank Ferguson. According to her texts, she had provided Frank with his statement to the press word for word.

The young woman looked so harmless and wholesome. Even sweet.

It was the dewy skin, the cute features and those damn pigtails.

"She won't crack," Brian said. "Believe me, I've tried."

Becca popped more nuts into her mouth, chewing and thinking.

"What were her exact words again, inside the house?" Rocco asked.

"Uh, something about it being too late. That no one could stop it."

They needed to find out what *it* was. Soon.

"How much time was left on the countdown on the laptop?" Jake asked.

"Can't be sure. It happened so fast. I only got a glimpse. Hours. Maybe two and change." Brian glanced at his watch. "If I'm right, that means we've got less than an hour left to figure it out."

"I could give it a go," Nash said, "and try talking to her."

Sheriff Daniel Clark folded his arms. "I'll go in with you. We could play good cop, bad cop. That might work."

"It might." Becca crumpled the empty bag and tossed it into the waste bin. "But not on that one." She gestured to Hannah.

Jake turned to her. "What are you thinking?"

"You and I play good cop, bad cop but with her godfather. Frank." She looked at Sheriff Clark. "Where is he?"

"Sitting in interrogation room 2."

"We use Hannah to break him." Becca stared at the woman again. "He never expected her to get caught or to suffer any consequences. Frank's big on family, community. Hell, he didn't do any of this for himself. He must be close with her."

"They're tight, for sure," Brian said. "Found several photos of them together. He even attended her graduation out at Cornell."

She nodded. "We use their bond to break him."

"It still won't hurt for us to have another go at her," Nash said. "She's been a data security analyst at Plainsman Oil and Gas for a year and half. There's no telling what kind of damage she's done."

In her gut, Becca knew it would be a waste of time. "Go for it." She gave a one-shoulder shrug. "You never know. She might want to brag about her handiwork."

"Rocco and I could try Troy Sims," Brian offered. "He might know. On pain meds, there's a better chance he'll let his guard down and let something slip."

"True. Provided he knows anything." She opened a bottle of water and took a sip. "I got the impression that Craig hadn't been in the loop on this. They may have cut Troy out of that part of the plan as well."

"Only one way to find out," Rocco said.

The three teams separated, each taking a perp to interrogate.

Inside interrogation room 2, Frank sat handcuffed to the metal table that was bolted down. He looked up at them as they entered and took seats across from them.

"Would you like some water?" Becca sat an ice-cold bottle down in front of him.

"That's funny." Frank's mouth hitched up in a half grin. "You offering me that, after I gave you so little."

"I don't hold grudges," she said. Which was lucky for Jake. No matter what he said wrong or how he messed up, she found herself able to forgive and forget and move on.

Now she wondered if they'd be able to move on, together, as a family.

"But I do." Jake glared at him. "Because of you we have quite a few people suffering from heat exhaustion and dehydration. Traumatized kids who'll need a lot of hours of therapy. And this fine agent here," he said, pointing at Becca, "could have been seriously injured or worse. And I intend to take it out on someone."

"Do your worst." Frank shrugged. "I'm a dead man walking, remember? If Lund's people don't kill me because Crispin doesn't want this rehashed in the media when it comes time for a trial, then heart failure will get me."

Aaron Vance had discovered that while Lund's head of security was in the Marines, he had attended the Corps' scout sniper school. Graduates were legendary for their tactical proficiency, as well as physical and mental toughness. A deputy had tracked him down to the Lund residence, where he had claimed to have been at the time of the shooting. Another security guard corroborated his story.

It angered Becca when horrible people got away with a crime. Dale McKee hadn't even been armed when he was shot and killed.

"Either way, my future is bleak," Frank added with a hint of a grin.

"Then why are you smiling?" Becca asked.

"Crispin may not have paid the money that a whole lot of people desperately need, but justice will be served. It won't be cold, either. It'll be red hot. And he'll deserve it."

"What's Hannah planning?" Jake asked, and Frank's smile fell from his face. "We have her in custody. That grudge I'm holding won't be taken out on you, but on her." Jake paused, and Becca suspected it was to let that sink a second. "We've seen the countdown. What happens when the time runs out? Are all the databases at Plainsman Oil and Gas going to be corrupted? Deleted?" Jake asked, fishing, but Frank's expression turned impassive. "Is it a bomb?"

The man's gaze fell, his body tensing as he chewed his lower lip.

"Frank," Becca said, "if people die—"

"No one is going to get killed." Frank clasped his hands. "Hannah made sure of that."

"Made sure how?" she asked. When he stayed silent, she said, "Nothing is foolproof. Sometimes people are in the wrong place at the wrong time. She's not God. Some things are beyond her control." That did nothing to motivate him to speak. "Whatever is going to happen won't be justice. It'll be vengeance."

Frank straightened, meeting her eyes. "If I can't have one, I'll settle for the other."

"Even at the expense of Hannah's future?" she asked.

The sudden tightness in his expression told her that he hadn't considered that.

"Once that bomb detonates," Jake said, "Hannah will be a domestic terrorist. If people are killed, you can add however many counts of murder to her rap sheet. You didn't think anyone would die when you took hostages. Look at how that turned out. Dale and Craig are dead. More people, innocent people, are going to die and Hannah will go to prison for it."

Chewing on his lower lip, Frank was mulling it over.

"Her Ivy League education will be virtually worthless," Becca said. "No more career. No bright future with a family of her own. Just a bleak one behind bars. Is that really what you want for her?"

A tortured look crossed his face.

"Is that what Marianne would want? For Hannah to sacrifice everything for vengeance?"

Tears leaked from the corner of one of his eyes.

"Is she going to blow up their headquarters? People work late there all the time." Now she was the one fishing, but nothing in his body language hinted that was the objective.

What else would they target that would cripple or financially ruin Plainsman?

It was an oil and gas company. *Think, Becca.* They had HAZMAT trucks, and rigs, and wells, and—"

"The oil reserves," Jake said.

Frank's gaze lowered again as he shifted in his seat.

That was it. But they needed to push harder to be sure. "The oil reserves are worth what? Hundreds of millions?" she asked.

"Try billions," Frank snapped. "It will bankrupt the company."

"Even if you succeeded at doing that, it would come at a devastating cost. Not only to Hannah but also the environment," Jake said. "But if we can get to it in time and disarm it, then this doesn't have to be the end for Hannah. She can still have a bright future. A wonderful life." Jake rested his forearms on the table. "How many bombs?"

"One. That's all that was needed. Everything at the depot is flammable. It'll all go boom, sky high. Burn up the air, maybe all the way to heaven."

Dear God.

Jake's jaw hardened. "Where exactly is the bomb set?"

"I don't know." Frank shook his head. "Dale was the one who planted it. Only he knew."

Jake cursed. "What about the detonator? Hannah triggered it, right?"

"Yeah. The first countdown is to set off the alarms in the facility."

"To evacuate the place," Becca guessed. "So no one gets hurt."

Frank nodded. "Then another countdown for the bomb. She created some kind of linked reactionary trigger. I don't know the technical name for it. The timer for the bomb won't start until the alarm does. I think she set it for twenty minutes. Enough time for folks to get out and away from the tank farm."

"Sometimes personnel will stay behind anyway," Jake said, "to manage the problem and try to get it under control. There might still be people on-site who could be killed. Can Hannah stop it?"

"I don't know." Frank's voice was despondent. "If it was possible, she'd never agree to do it."

Becca pushed curls from her face, tucking the strands behind her ear. "Why not?"

"Once Hannah commits, she goes all in. Hard. Been that way ever since she was a little girl. It won't matter what you threaten her with. The girl is stubborn."

Jake stood. "How far is the depot from here?"

"The tank farm is a thirty-minute drive," Frank said. "Out toward Centennial."

Becca checked the time on the clock on the wall. "Thank you, Frank." They left the room and went into the hall. "We've got to hurry." She closed the door to the interrogation room, calculating how much time might be left until the alarm started. Then the countdown for the bomb. "We'll be cutting it close."

Frowning, Jake opened his mouth. "I don't think that you should—"

"Finish that statement and you'll regret it, Delgado." She put her hands on her hips. "I think you're forgetting that I'm more qualified to go out there on this one than you are. I'm far from being an expert but I did take a course at Quantico on explosive ordnance disposal. Can you say the same?" she asked, and he shook his head once, his lips pressed in a thin, tight line. "Then instead of being a jerk, be a partner with me on this. We finish it together. As a team. Okay?"

He didn't look happy about it, but he said, "Okay. Together."

She turned to go gather the others, but he put a hand on her shoulder, drawing her back to him.

"Hey," he said, pulling her close. He ran his hand over her hair and cupped her cheek. "No matter what happens out there, I want you to know that I respect you. Always have. It wasn't just sex for me. While you were held hostage, I realized that it was more for me, too."

He pressed his lips to hers. The kiss was quick, yet tender and tantalizing, his lips so soft and warm that she wanted to melt into him. She pulled back and saw in his eyes that he wanted to do more, say more, but they had a job to do.

This man was her storm and her sanctuary.

How could one person be both?

But he was Jake, and it was complicated.

She prayed they'd get a chance to delve deeper into their feelings and whether anything was possible for them as a couple. For now... "Let's go stop a bomb."

They hurried down the hall side by side.

"Was the course you took an advanced one?" he asked.

How she wished that it had been. "Afraid not. As it stands, I know enough not to set the sucker off."

He chuckled under his breath. "Well, it's still a heck of a lot more than I know. I only hope it's enough."

Chapter Sixteen

Jake had reached out to the SWAT commander, Utley, and requested that their explosives expert accompany them to the oil depot. An entire bomb squad with a bunch of dogs trained to sniff out explosive devices would have been better. But one police specialist and one FBI agent who had at the very least taken an EOD course would have to suffice.

En route, they had called the depot, reaching the night manager. No alarm had started yet. Nash had given orders to evacuate and clear the site.

But by the time their convoy of law enforcement vehicles arrived at the storage depot, the facility's alarm was blaring—a loud *whoop-whoop* siren along with clanging bells. The countdown for the bomb had started.

They parked their SUVs in front of the first of five enormous warehouses that had large rolling steel doors, most likely to allow for trucks. The buildings were shaped like massive air hangars. He had no idea how many tanks were stored in each or how long it would take them to search all five.

Beads of sweat rolled down his spine. Jake was betting that Becca's nerves were as raw as his.

"I'm the night manager!" a tall, lanky man shouted over the alarm as he approached them.

"I'm Supervisory Special Agent Garner," Nash said over the earsplitting noise. "What are you still doing here?"

The manager adjusted the white hard hat on his head. "Thought you might need me."

"Can you shut off the alarm?" Jake asked, needing to raise his voice. The combination of the siren and bells was horrendous. Which was also the point to get people to evacuate. But for their purpose, a person couldn't hear themselves think with the racket. How was someone supposed to disarm a bomb?

The manager shook his head. "Already tried! We've got no control over it. Like someone hacked into the system or something. Oddest thing."

"How long has it been going off?" Becca asked.

"About fifteen minutes!"

That gave them less than five to stop it.

Jeez. Were they going to make it when they had five facilities to search?

"We're looking for an explosive device that's been in place for at least a couple of days," the SWAT expert, Stevens, said. "It's going to be somewhere that wouldn't be easy to spot. Can you think of any places inside the buildings where that might be?"

"Doubtful it would be on a storage tank," the manager shouted. "We spot-check those every day. Control panels, too." He looked like he was thinking.

"Hate to rush you," Jake said, "but we need to hurry."

Flustered, the manager froze.

Jake swore the air pulsed with heat. The humidity was heavy, making Becca's hair even curlier.

"Maybe the generators?" the manager finally said. "They're large steel boxes. You could put something inside of them. We only check those when we do quarterly maintenance. Three generators for each unit. One in the front, the middle, and the back."

Stevens turned to everyone. "Split up! Each team take a warehouse." He called out a number that corresponded to the one on the hangar door and pointed to a team. "If you find the device, let me know. I'll come to you and disarm it. Stay alert. Stay alive."

Everyone nodded and took off for their respective storage facility.

The warehouses were so enormous, that it was faster to get back into the SUV and drive to the ones farther away.

Jake got behind the wheel. Becca hopped into the passenger's seat. They sped down to storage unit number three, the one smack-dab in the middle. He slammed on the brakes, kicking up dust, and threw the vehicle in Park while Rocco and Brian, in a different SUV, kept going, and the sheriff along with a deputy headed for the final one.

Becca and Jake jumped out. They raced to the main door and dashed inside.

The temperature dropped twenty degrees. Too bad the cool air wasn't a relief. The alarms were still screeching, making his head pound.

"There's the first one." Becca pointed to the corner.

They ran to it. The unit was at least sixty by forty by forty. There was a door on the right side. He pulled it open. Crouching down, he swung the beam of a flashlight inside. Everything appeared as it should, but there was one spot he couldn't see.

"Other side back corner," he said to Becca, jerking his head in the direction. "Check for another door."

She rushed around the unit and took a look. "No door, but there's a panel. Do you have anything I can use to take out a screw?"

Jake dug into his pocket and pulled out his Swiss Army multi-tool knife. He tossed it to her.

She caught it, knelt and started working on the screw. He double-checked to make sure he hadn't missed anything.

Stevens had not told them what size device they should be looking for.

Becca removed the panel. Light shone in from the other side, illuminating the dark corner. "Clear," she said.

They were up on their feet, moving to find the next one. Running past tanks with bright white and red labels that read Combustible, No Smoking, they were reminded of the danger. One explosive device would take out the entire tank farm, killing everyone in the vicinity.

Once they reached the center of the massive facility, they looked around.

"Over there." Jake led the way to the unit that was tucked off to the side.

There was an alarm with flashing lights mounted on

the wall right overhead. Their proximity magnified the already deafening noise.

As he opened the door and shined the light around, Becca put the multi-tool to good use on the other side, removing the screws to the back panel.

The steel plate fell to the floor.

"Got it. I can see the bomb from here."

He'd barely made out what she said through the shrill clanging.

Jake got up and dashed around to her side. Dropping to a knee next to Becca, he spotted the small black metal container about the size and shape of a bread box.

He got on comms. "We've located a device."

Would they be able to hear him over the blaring noise?

Using the long, flat blade, Becca stuck the tip beneath the lip of the container and began prying it up, slowly.

"Where?" Stevens responded.

Jake realized he hadn't identified himself. "This is Delgado. Warehouse 3."

Becca got the lid of the black box open.

"Repeat! Can't hear."

Damn it.

"Definitely homemade," Becca said. "Not sophisticated. Thank You, Lord."

"Warehouse 3," Jake repeated. "Homemade device located."

"They probably got this off the internet," Becca said. "Maybe from a book. Which is good for us."

Please be simple. Please be simple.

"Headed your way." Stevens said something else, but Jake couldn't make it out over the alarm. "Do nothing."

"Where's the timer?" Jake asked.

"There." Becca pointed to a display with blinking red digits, but they were covered by wires. She slipped the flat side of the blade under the pair of wires, red and blue twisted together. Leaning forward, she cupped her hand around the small screen to make it easier to read. "Thirty-five seconds."

He sucked in a ragged breath.

"We do nothing, we die," she said.

"Well, do something." Anything. Stevens wouldn't reach them in time, and he trusted Becca. "Less than thirty seconds before it explodes," he said over comms. "Clear out!" If they couldn't be saved, maybe the others still had a chance to hightail it a safe distance away.

Jake looked at the timer over her shoulder.

Twenty-eight seconds. Twenty-seven.

He watched Becca untwist the wires and follow each one to its lead. His heart threatened to beat out of his chest.

Nineteen seconds. Eighteen.

Time condensed into an excruciating moment. Yet Jake felt each ticking second as though it was a distinct unit. Each one a separate universe of time while also slipping from one into the next.

Ten, nine.

They were almost out of time. He struggled to keep the panic clawing through him at bay.

Seven, six.

He wanted to tell Becca he loved her. That he was sorry for all his mistakes. His mouth was opening—

"Ready or not," she said, holding the scissors.

He watched, transfixed, as she snipped the green wire. His gaze fell to the display screen.

Two seconds left on the clock.

His breath whooshed from his mouth. Sweet relief suffused every pore.

The alarm finally stopped with a small squawk. All was silent besides the hammering of his pulse in his ears.

They were alive. Becca had done it.

This amazing woman he loved.

When the heck it had happened, he couldn't say for sure. But just as they were about to die, he'd been certain.

Jake reached out and wiped away the line of perspiration streaming down Becca's cheek. "You did great for one class, sweetheart. You were right—"

There was a loud pop.

They both froze. Then they peered into the box.

Another pop came from the black metal container. It almost sounded like bang snap novelty fireworks.

Jake didn't move. He didn't even breathe.

Becca bent over and examined the disarmed explosive device. At least he prayed it was completely defused.

"One of the leads sparked." She lifted the wire, touched the tip with her fingers and set it on the floor. "I figured it was best to get it away from the dynamite."

He nodded, his tension deflating. "Are we good?"

"It won't blow us sky high." Smiling, she sat back on her heels. "So, yeah, we're good."

A litany of things that he wanted to say to her, now

that they had time, rushed into his head. He didn't know where to start. "Becca, relationships are ugly and complicated and messy. More so for an agent, much less for two trying to do it together."

Her brow furrowed. "What are you saying?"

The door to the hangar opened. Footsteps pounded, heading their way.

"I'm saying I love you. I want the baby." Beneath the fear and anxiety had been a bone-deep love for their child after he heard its heartbeat. "I want there to be an us. Ugly, complicated mess and all. I just don't want to disappoint you."

She leaned closer and caressed his face. "The only way you could ever disappointment me is by giving up."

"Is it still armed?" Stevens yelled as he ran toward them.

"No, Becca disarmed it!"

Stevens stopped, still a good ten yards away, and hauled in a deep breath.

Jake laughed at the craziness that was their life. One they were going to have together. With a baby.

He looked back at her. "No worries about me ever giving up," he said. "Once I'm committed, I don't quit."

Four days later

As BECCA STUCK THE key in the lock of her condo, Jake glanced at his watch.

"We're late," he said. "The sheriff told us to tune in at noon for his big statement to the press."

"They were backed up at the doctor's office." Opening the door, they went in. She welcomed the cool air. "The doctor ran behind, making us late. Nothing we can do about it."

But she was glad Jake had taken a week off to spend with her and had been there at the appointment.

He strode into the living room and flipped on the TV. Dropping her purse on the coffee table, Becca sat beside him and put a hand on his thigh. She loved the feel of his lean, strong muscles.

"Crispin Lund has been taken into custody thanks to the evidence his wife provided regarding a hydrofracking accident that happened two years ago," the sheriff said on the screen. "As a result of that tragedy, many employees and residents near the site have gotten ill. Some have died. What Crispin Lund did by covering it up was heinous. I am also reopening the cold case on Jennifer Paulson. She was a board member of Plainsman Oil and Gas Company. After agreeing to help the would-be claimants in a potential class action lawsuit, she died under mysterious circumstances. I will do everything to see her murderer brought to justice. Mrs. Lund has asked to make a brief statement."

"I guess not doing everything in his power to spare Cameron any suffering was the last straw for her," Jake said.

"Money meant more than the welfare of his son." Becca shook her head. "Unbelievable."

"I'm sure that's how his wife felt."

Mrs. Lund appeared on the screen with her son, Cameron, and Father O'Neill, standing beside her. "My heart breaks for this community. I am ashamed and appalled by my husband's actions. After I found the evidence that confirmed everything that I'd heard about the industrial accident, I knew that my silence, my inaction, would have made me complicit. That is why I have come forward. To aid those in their fight for justice. I learned that many families signed a nondisclosure agreement that would prevent them from joining a new class action lawsuit. Therefore, I am in the process of establishing a fund for them in the amount of seven million dollars, to assist them with their medical bills and living expenses. I know this doesn't atone for the sins of our family. But I pray that it is a good start."

Jake turned off the TV. "That's incredible."

"I hope it brings Frank some peace."

"After what those men put you through, I'm amazed by how sympathetic you are."

"They were desperate. With no other recourse. I don't agree with their methods, but I understand what they must have felt, being caught between a rock and a hard place. Wanting justice. Not being able to get it."

"If the evidence Mrs. Lund provided is legitimate, then they'll get it. And even though they might not be able to file a class action lawsuit due to the NDA, there's no reason the families of those who died can't file a wrongful death suit." He leaned back on the sofa and tipped his head up. "Hey, did they ever find Abigail Abshire?"

"Nope. But I'm not sure how hard they're looking." Becca reached for her purse and pulled out the picture of the sonogram her OB had printed for them. She couldn't stop staring at the image of their baby.

Getting up, she headed for the fridge. She grabbed a magnet and hung up the sonogram.

The second ultrasound with Jake had been ten times better than the first. Once he had decided to be all-in with her and the little one on the way, he seemed to focus less on worrying and more on problem-solving.

Like how they were going to live in Fort Collins, Colorado, near the border of Wyoming. From there they would both have a manageable, albeit very long, commute to work until she could put in for a transfer to Denver. She loved working on the joint task force and living close to her sister, but she wanted to start a family with Jake even more. His parents lived in Fort Collins. His mother was still a homemaker, and his father was about to retire. They were ready to move mountains if it meant they could spend time with their first grandchild.

Her sister as well as his sister would only be an hour away.

The plan they'd come up with was a huge relief.

Jake came up alongside her, pulling her into his arms. He lowered his head and kissed her.

Her heart leaped the second his lips touched hers. His fingers tightened on the back of her neck and his other arm wrapped around her waist, tugging her closer in an embrace that was so delicious she never wanted it to end.

The well-muscled hardness of his body pressed against hers had raw need flooding her.

He eased back. "Are you sure you don't want to marry me?"

She wanted more kisses, more touching, more laughter. More of Jake. "I didn't say I didn't want to. I said let's take it slow. Have the baby. Make sure we don't kill each other in a sleep-deprived rage first."

They both laughed.

His expression turned serious. "You're not sure about me?"

Although they would still fight, especially as new parents and eventually as newlyweds, she was also convinced that they would never stop fighting *for* their relationship.

"Oh, no. I'm one hundred percent positive about you. About us." Ever since they were cadets at Quantico, she'd believed that if he could get his act together in the romance department, he would be one hell of a catch. Now that he was hers, she wasn't letting go. "This feels right."

"Yeah, it does. We're building something *real* together." He grinned at her with love gleaming in his eyes. "Can I at least buy you a ring? We can have a long engagement."

She smiled at him. "I think I can be persuaded."

"Happy to hear that we can make this official, because I've had a thing for you since the academy," he said.

"Ditto."

"Oh yeah? Why didn't you ever tell me?"

It hadn't been the right time. Not until now. "You didn't have a need to know."

Chuckling, he glanced at the sonogram. "I can't wait until we find out the sex."

"What do you want? A boy or girl?"

"It doesn't matter. Just a healthy baby."

Even his responses had gone from annoying to perfect. "Me, too."

"And an easy delivery for you, Old Mama." He smacked her behind.

She elbowed him in the ribs. Almost perfect responses. "Watch it, Delgado."

"Have I ever told you that I hate it when you call me Delgado?"

Becca gave a knowing smile. "No, you haven't." She had already figured as much. "But I've got to keep you in line some kind of way."

"I suppose you do. Nobody else has been able to."

He leaned in and the kiss he gave her filled her with such sweet warmth, the sensation spreading through her like sinking into a warm bath, and she knew their love—their marriage one day—would last a lifetime.

* * * * *

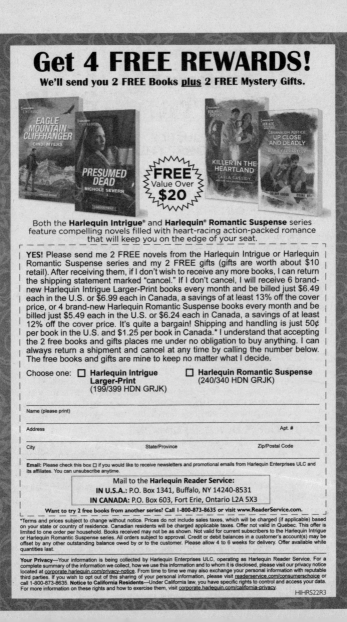

HARLEQUIN
PLUS

Try the best multimedia subscription service for romance readers like you!

Read, Watch and Play.

Experience the easiest way to get the romance content you crave.

Start your **FREE TRIAL** at
www.harlequinplus.com/freetrial.